THE S CODE

AF080989

PRANEETH REMIDI

BlueRoseONE
Stories Matter
NewDelhi • London

BLUEROSE PUBLISHERS
India | U.K.

Copyright © Praneeth Remidi 2024

All rights reserved by author. No part of this publication may be reproduced, stored in a retrieval system or transmitted in any form or by any means, electronic, mechanical, photocopying, recording or otherwise, without the prior permission of the author. Although every precaution has been taken to verify the accuracy of the information contained herein, the publisher assume no responsibility for any errors or omissions. No liability is assumed for damages that may result from the use of information contained within.

BlueRose Publishers takes no responsibility for any damages, losses, or liabilities that may arise from the use or misuse of the information, products, or services provided in this publication.

For permissions requests or inquiries regarding this publication, please contact:

BLUEROSE PUBLISHERS
www.BlueRoseONE.com
info@bluerosepublishers.com
+91 8882 898 898
+4407342408967

ISBN: 978-93-5989-744-8

Cover design: Tahira
Typesetting: Tanya Raj Upadhyay

First Edition: February 2024

"To my beloved wife, Vanisree, my unwavering support.

This novel is dedicated to you. Without you I could not have ventured into unconventional works."

Introduction

'Why do stories emerge in me and why do I attempt to write them?' It's a question that often weaves its way into my thoughts as I navigate the realms of storytelling. I don't aspire to turn writing into a career, nor do I seek any gains beyond the occasional praise from friends and a handful of readers within my circle. Yet, I take out time to patiently translate my thoughts onto paper, questioning whether this act is a blessing or a curse.

Upon reflection, I realize that my subconscious is fueled by the profound impact of a select few books, such as 'Mahaprasthanam' by Sri Sri and 'Geethanjali' by Rabindranath Tagore, alongside the timeless wisdom of Swami Vivekananda and the captivating novels of Yandamoori Virendranath. The Telugu movie songs from my childhood, infused with rich literary values, have had a significant impact on my appreciation for description.

These literary treasures have nestled themselves in the deep corners of my mind. They surface constantly in my thoughts without my conscious intervention - those writings are like a bee locked and buzzing in my mind's room. These literary expressions might have shaped my worldview with newfound empathy. That is why I see a worthy story in every object, in every person, and in every situation, then I proceed to narrate.

In the tapestry of my imagination, countless stories find their place — some woven into bedtime tales for my daughter, others shared over evening snacks with my wife and a few glimpses revealed at parties with friends. Yet, once in a rare while, a narrative like 'The S Code' emerges, a story meant not just for my close circle but for the world at large. It's a tale that demanded to be published, compelling me to share its intrigue and depth with readers everywhere.

'The S Code,' is a narrative that unfolds between 1945 and 2008, with a significant portion rooted in the transformative year of 1985. Far from a meticulously planned story, 'The S code' emerged organically from a single thought: 'What if a young farmer stumbled upon a vast treasure while tilling the soil?' This fictional narrative, non-linear in its progression, is an authentic evolution of that initial scene.

'The S Code' is a story I allowed to unravel naturally over time and is a narrative I patiently nurtured for years. I am overwhelmed by the unfolding of this tale, believing that the story itself chose me as a vessel for its revelation. My role was merely to transcribe it as it unveiled itself to me.

Much like the letter 'S' with its turns and twists, 'The S Code' encapsulates a captivating journey of treasure, from its inception to its conclusion.

Thank you for embarking on this journey with me!

Prologue

In the year around 1965, in the modest backyard of the tile-roofed house, the mother gently swayed on a jute-woven cot, her 8-year-old son Naagam nestled in the cradle of her arms. Under the vast canvas of the summer night adorned with countless stars, the nightly ritual of bedtime stories began. But on that day, the discourse initiated by the son was not anticipated by his mother.

'Mother, is it true that there are twenty-one treasure jars hidden in the forest?' Naagam inquired, his voice a soft murmur among the rhythmic chirping of distant crickets.

'Yes child, but who told you this?' his mother responded, her hand gently stroking his hair and her eyes fixed on the sky.

'My friends mentioned it, and I overheard people discussing it near the drinking water well,' he replied, finding comfort in his mother's soothing touch.

'But why could they found only one after all these years?' He asked.

'No one knows exactly where they were hidden in the vast forest and the one they found was near the Rishi Pahar mountain.' the mother explained patiently, her fingers tracing circles on Naagam's back.

'There is a code, it seems, so why can't they find it?' Naagam questioned, his curiosity piqued.

'Because no one has been able to decipher the code,' she replied fighting against the drowsiness.

'I will decode it, Mother. I will work hard to find at least one treasure jar,' Naagam declared with innocence and determination.

'My dear Naagam, one should not squander time searching for something uncertain. Instead, work hard and earn money. Treasure is a matter of luck.'

'I will work hard and simultaneously search for treasure, then. Is that okay, Mother?' he asked, his voice loud and confident.

'How can you do both?' she inquired, a fond smile playing on her lips.

'Once I grow up, I shall take up beekeeping like Father does. I will search for treasure near and around every Arjuna tree.'

'Why specifically the Arjuna tree?' his mother inquired while curiosity invaded her drowsiness.

'People say that, according to the code, the probability of finding treasure is near and around the old Arjuna trees.' The boy's answer was quick.

'How about the snake? It comes to fight if you got the treasure,' the mother posed the question.

'I will pray to it to go away, with the sacred band of Lord Shiva coiled around my wrist,' he responded with a touch of naivety and confidence.

Since 1945, the year when soldiers sacrificed their lives to protect the treasure, these kinds of conversation echoed through time, resonating in homes, streets, and dedicated gatherings. For the people living in the villages near the Naimisha forest, these discussions fueled their curiosity to venture into the woods in search of the guarded wealth. This era of discourse, curiosity, and adventure continued for sixty-five years.

Table of Contents

Stumbled upon legacy sealed in brass 1

The submissive king and the radiant beauty 17

The Sinister Scheme and the Sacrifice 42

The igniting story of bee keeper 73

Revolt and conspiracy – Hand in hand 95

Revealing the buried fortune 147

The Revenge Plan 171

The S Code mystery 204

Epilogue: What is S code 211

Stumbled upon legacy sealed in brass

In 2008 at the summer end on 06th June
28yearold Aditya was tilling the land to prepare it for the next season

A big iron ring of a long strong chain struck to the plough share handled by Aditya, the son of the late Vijaya Raghava. The bulls were struggling to pull the plough but they could not forward an inch and were motionless; usually, a rock or the large, hard, and condensed soil lumps make the plough burden by obstructing it; in such cases, as everyone does, Aditya tried to lift the handle a little from the mud to shake it if not to displace it but of no use, he could not lift it an inch at least. Adjusting the shirt's sleeves and pulling the jeans short up and tight, he ensured his Nokia mobile was safe in the short's pocket. Rounding the bullwhips to the plough handle, Aditya bent down to check what obstructed the plough. Nothing did he notice at the immediate sight but then as he knelt on one knee and examined by cleaning the mud around the plough, the sight of the big iron ring with a chain passed through the thin long triangular shaft of the plough, made him almost go numb. Tremors like shivers shot through his spine and shocked his body, his heart started to race at its maximum, like never before, as if he was running miles to escape from a hungry wild animal's hunt. His thoughts went frozen and his eyes blurred. His mouth went dry and his skin senseless. A moment before, he had been tilling the soil to prepare the field for the next season to cultivate cotton, till a moment back, the irritation of the end summer heat added with the loo blows had been pinching him throughout the body except for the feet which was ruptured by the utter dry chunks of black soil on the field. But the sight of the ring surpassed the summer wind that had been pinching him; the feet ruptured by the dry chunks were not at all in consideration. He was not aware that minutes were passing by as he still knelt beside the plough and was lost in the thoughts of the ever-anxious and jarring experience. His heart was pounding so much that the ribs felt it. His breath was becoming short and the silence was so scary to his veins – the God's blaring siren before the earth's collapse would be little better than it - but yes, the witnessing of the combination – iron ring with strong chain - is worth for sure of all that momentous experience and especially for Aditya. The iron ring of a long strong chain is the most familiar word in the village of Jhagaaram. The legends, his father and uncle's missing mystery and folklore confirm the presence of the treasure chest a few feet deep if the iron ring with a long chain is found. The treasure chest was a brass jar holding the gold jewelry anywhere between seventy to eighty kilo grams, few packets of diamonds, pearls - and hence, not a surprise for anyone to go blank in senses by witnessing the wonder and imagining the consequences.

His father flashed across his mind, who went missing when he was eight and not just the mystery of his father's missing but there was a mystery of history around this which led to one of the significant movements 'Shivan's Pride' in the region. His father played a crucial role in the 'Shivan's Pride' movement and later when he went missing, Aditya too for a while tried to be active in the movement when he was in his teens but the movement got diluted by that time.

Calm, composed, and way more mature than his age, Aditya had a lot to do with the treasure than anyone else in the world at that time.

'Let me confirm it first.' Saying to himself, he touched the iron ring to believe what he saw and scribbled his hand into the mud along the chain to confirm that it was of some length. Holding the chain with two hands, he pulled it with all his strength but of no use.

'No doubt, it's a treasure chest here in the brass jar.' Aditya had been struggling to confirm his state between the reality and dream. He looked around and found none at sight. The sky was burning for the eyes to look at it. The day was about to get into noon. What does anyone do if realized a treasure! The story of Naagam flashed in his mind despite his state of mind.

'Hey Aditya,' he heard a cry from an acquaintance passing on the bicycle along the road towards the town, 'let's meet in the evening at the GOST troop play.' He went away without expecting any response. GOST - troop was an abbreviation of Guardians of Shivan's Tale.

The four acres field is located on the road side corner of the Jhagaram village, the village was one of the prominent villages in the area for three reasons - the presence of Rishi Pahar Mountain - for being adjacent to one of the densest forests - for being in the erstwhile kingdom of Vijetha mandala.

Hearing the cry from the acquaintance, Aditya released the chain in his hand and realized that he had to first move away from the spot and anything and everything was next, lest anyone noticed. He tried his hands, pulling the ring away from the plough share but their circumferences overlapped tight and the ring fastened the plough. Had he forced the bulls, they would pull the Jar to the surface but that is not what Aditya wanted. He planned the status quo for the treasure. Before another bicycle passed by, Aditya wanted to move away from the spot. He found a big rock within a few meters, tightening the bull whips on the plough handle he picked it up. The bulls had the habit of walking towards the owner but before they acted, Aditya swiftly jumped back with the rock. It wasn't difficult for him to beat the iron ring and separate it. Using his feet for a while and then his hands, he dug a few inches to hide back the iron ring and the chain. He then walked straight towards the boundary of his field by counting the number of steps which ended at forty-four till the nearest boundary. He then took right at the boundary to sit under the neem tree without forgetting to count again in his right direction which again added twenty-six more steps. So, if to find the spot of treasure jar he had to stand at the neem tree and walk towards his right for twenty-six steps and then turn left to take forty-four steps more.

'Twenty-six and forty-four, let me remember it like two six double four, two six double four.' He started to chant gazing at the spot.

It was eleven in the morning and an hour more for Aditya to get back from the field. During the summers, the farmers reached the field by six in the morning and worked till noon and they called it a day. Very rarely and only if urgent, they worked in the late evenings.

Aditya rested the plough and released the bulls to feed them water in the storage tank adjacent to the tree. The bulls sat down and started grazing the hay under the tree shade. On a bump on the surface under the tree, Aditya was not consistent in his seating.

The folklores, the stories, the legend, and the witnesses say that deep in the woods and across the woods - there were twenty-one chests with seventy kilograms of gold each – the gold in the form of coins, chains, bracelets, rings and a few had pearls and might be some diamonds too. But a treasure jar hidden in the field had something to do with the missing story of his father, Raghava, and his father's friend, Vikram.

Every kid raised in the village knew the stories of treasure as early as they knew 'The lion and the Mouse' and everyone dreamed of finding one and also venturing for adventures. Aditya was no different except that the recent few years he had no hopes of getting a chest as his immersion in the business of sanitary ware bent his mind to approach life practically. The practicality of life negates the less probable – the finding of the brass jar is undoubtedly the least probability for a person, though the proportionate worth of it deserves the efforts of the entire village for at least their life time.

Unable to decide on how to go ahead Aditya spent more than an hour just gazing at the treasure spot. For all the time he sat there he only tried to calm his mind and heart while his subconscious mind sprayed events that haunted him for years.

'The legends and the code point to these treasures being hidden in the forest,' he mused, 'so how on earth did one of them end up here, in my field? It must be related to my father's disappearance, no doubt about it.' These puzzling circumstances intensified his determination to uncover the truth and he felt that the treasure itself chose him to reveal the truth.

He also recollected the code – The Shivan's code - which was in the form of a story by the soldiers who buried the treasure chests – *'Upon reaching Rishi Pahar Mountain, we beseeched Lord Shiva for his divine aid. Answering our plea, Lord Shiva appeared with a bow as high as the sky and concealed the treasures using the mountain-sized massive serpent as his arrow. The serpent clutched all the treasure jars with its fangs, and upon Lord Shiva's command, it sailed through the forest, secreting away the treasures deep under the soil, with the iron ring few inches below the ground. The clue to find the spots is the number 707.'*

Not only the code, but he was also reminded by a follow-up legend that anyone who noticed the treasure would be haunted by the same snake residing in the same mountain - *Anyone who dares to use this treasure for personal gain, the same serpent will haunt them. It will haunt them in their dreams and then they wake up to see the serpent coming so close that it licks their cheeks with its venomous fangs, coils around their necks and chests, crushing them until they gasp for breath, and it becomes their relentless torment until their last breath.*

Waited till the regular time to return, Aditya started from the field towards his house following the plough led by the bulls. He was determined to be usual and extra vigilant in his behavior and actions as it was the only opportunity he had to solve the mystery of his father's demise and correct the course of the history of the soldier's sacrifice.

His house was at the other end of the village from the field; hence he had to walk through the main street that covers half of the houses. Along the street was Raki's house where he usually stopped for a moment to check if he was at home.

'Raki, Raki.' He shouted to call him.

'Hmm, you are late from the field today, hope you are enjoying the work dude.' Rakesh spoke, coming out with the food plate in his hand.

'Enjoying? Does anyone enjoy this heat? So, tell me, what's the program after lunch' Aditya said while the bulls walked away. They were perfectly aware of the route.

'Nothing, TV awaits me as usual. Shall we meet after lunch then?'

'Ok, shall inform if anything, bye.' He left and was happy that his routine was not missed in anxiety nor Rakesh did notice any wrong in his behavior.

Aditya was born and brought up in the village of Jhagaaram. The school in the nearby village educated him. Could be a learning disorder, less severe - dyslexia, because of which Aditya never made it good in academics despite his sincere, ambitious and intended efforts. However, decisiveness, maturity and calmness were his attributes but none of these were neither intended nor by training. All of those attributes were half hereditary and the other was due to the circumstances after he lost his father when he was eight years of age. Like his father, he too was sought after for any leadership role in the school or college or any informal setting. In a large compound but in a proportionately small house, he lived with his paternal grandmother and his mother. With a huge backyard, unlike houses in Jhagaram, house of Aditya was big enough to fit for three to four families. Hence for every purpose, there was a dedicated room. The wash area, the toilet blocks, and the bathrooms were separated by a few yards from the house structure. Much of the large compound was dedicated to the backyard as it had a shed at one of its ends to accommodate two bulls, three buffaloes and the basic necessities like water and hay was arranged for them. The used water, wetting the three mango trees and one lemon tree along the way in the compound, flowed into the drainage line of the village. The rest of the area was used to grow seasonal vegetables; people in Jhagaram hardly shop vegetables.

Many of the existing house structures were built in the beginning of the village formation but underwent many repairs and overhauls. The roofs were mostly made of clay tiles in S shape that overlapped to form grip and stopped any rain water from dripping. As the families expanded through the generations, they started adding the rooms inside the compound and very few families built new houses.

The floor of Aditya's house looked modern comparatively. Twenty years back, after his father's demise, it was dug by the police in the presence of the revenue department and the villagers as they doubted that the treasure was hidden underground. Later, the family constructed a new floor.

Aditya parked the bulls in the shed and ensured the bulls had sufficient hay and water.

'Are you Okay.' Aditya's mother asked at his immediate sight while he was cleaning the mud off his hands and legs.

'How come mothers notice the slightest changes in behavior?' He thought for himself and asked her 'Why maa, am I not looking as usual.' Aditya sought confirmation from his mother and he was still cleaning his hands as the mud that got stuck in the nails was not easy to remove.

'Yes, but you seem lost in thoughts and let the bulls alone reach home.'

'Met Rakesh on the way and bulls continued their path.'

'When do you get Vandana here, it's been two weeks she has been with her parents, this is not good.' The mother said while serving a plate full of rice and brought the bowls of tomato curry, daal and rasam.

'Why is it not good, she didn't meet them for months before?' Said Aditya and trying to distract the topic that had been an everyday issue, he asked 'Did granny eat anything today.' He enquired about his granny who had been bedridden for a year due to old age.

'Little better today, served mashed rice and daal. Doctor has given intravenous fluid in the morning.' She replied.

'But she is really great maa, must be nearing her eighties, right? Had she not injured her leg, she would have been active even now.' Aditya said as he finished his plate.

'The kind of food they ate, the physical work they did kept them healthy. People those days used to climb the Rishi Pahar Mountain easily.' Rishi Pahar is a mountain located in the forest at an elevation of nearly six hundred meters with a breadth of five hundred meters.

'I know, basically in search of the treasure they did it right?' Aditya wanted to extract some information on the secrets of treasure.

'Who knew where the treasure is?' She spoke as she started cleaning the floor by removing the utensils and residuals.

'Didn't Father tell anything on treasure to you maa or are you hiding something?' Aditya raised the discussion which he usually did and his mother too usually avoided.

'Your father never had time to talk. He didn't say anything about treasure to me. Even if he had revealed something, I would not tell you ok.' The reply was a repetitive one.

'But tell me Mother, though it's been so many years, why no one can find the treasure except Nagam?'

'Will you stop talking about treasure?' The statement would shut Aditya's mouth and the mother continued, 'How about the shop? You cannot leave it completely to the workers. You need to visit every day.'

'Maa, you need not worry about it. It has already given our investment back and we are in profits with this.' He replied and walked to wash his hand that mixed all the yummy dishes. Aditya had started a business of sanitary ware products distribution that covered eight blocks in the district. As the business dealt with dealers, there was standardized-operational-procedures. The manager of the shop received the orders from the dealers and ensured they were dispatched in the next two days. The stock was updated weekly to the main distributor who dumps the required products accordingly. Aditya visited the shop every other day for two to three hours, coordinating primarily through mobile communication.

This was done intentionally because Aditya wanted to establish and sustain standard operating procedures for the business so that he could venture into another.

Aditya rested on the jute-woven wooden cot for the routine after lunch to watch the television and simultaneously chat with Vandana, his loving wife.

'Again, the mobile and the TV.' His mother's statement, while crossing his room, was so predictable that it never made it to touch the intended ears.

As every day, Aditya was on the same jute woven wooden cot, the same Nokia mobile and the same TV set but not the same state of mind. He wanted to inform his treasure news to Vandana or Rakesh or his mother but ceased himself, he firmly believed that two can keep a secret if one of them is dead. His brain started sending plans to unleash the treasure; all his instincts indicated his immediate action on that night but he promised to himself that he wouldn't take any action hastily and not to repeat the mistakes others did. His logic was simple - any hasty decision would expose the treasure news to the world but inaction was safe.

It's not an ordinary treasure, not even easy to calculate the worth without a calculator.

'How much is seventy kilograms of gold' he started converting but before that he needed to know the value of one gram. As he was immersed in recollecting his knowledge, the Nokia mobile rang in Chall chayya chayya ringtone.

'Aditya,' Vandana spoke in a hesitant tone.

'Yes, Vandana, tell me, how are you? I missed your call in the morning. Thought of calling you but could not,' Aditya said in a low and tired tone.

Vandana paused for a moment, her voice trembling slightly as she continued, 'Aditya, I went to the doctor today.'

Concerned Aditya got up off the cot, the calculator on his Nokia mobile forgotten for the moment. 'The doctor? Is everything alright?'

Vandana's voice grew even softer, and she hesitated before replying, 'Aditya, I'm not unwell.'

'What? Then why did you visit the doctor? Are you mad or what?' worried Aditya.

'Yes, when the doctor confirmed that I'm pregnant.'

Aditya's eyes widened, and he felt a mix of emotions – surprise, joy, and a touch of anxiety. 'Pregnant? Vandana, that's... that's a great news!'

Vandana managed a shy smile on the other end of the line. 'I know.'

Aditya's heart warmed at Vandana's words. 'I'm really sorry I missed your call earlier. It's been a tough day at work, and I was caught up with some issues.'

'It's okay, Aditya. I understand,' Vandana reassured him. 'But there's one more thing.'

Aditya, curious and eager, asked, 'What is it, Vandana?'

Vandana hesitated once more, her shyness evident in her voice as she said, 'Could you please share the news with Aunty.' Vandana felt shy about sharing this with Aditya's mother.

Aditya felt a sudden shyness creeping in as well. 'Um, Vandana, I... I'm not comfortable sharing this with Amma, that's women's talk, you can tell her directly.'

Vandana understood Aditya's feelings and agreed, 'Of course, Aditya. No problem at all.'

With a sense of relief, Aditya handed the phone to his mother, who was in the kitchen. 'Vandana wants to talk to you, Amma.'

Aditya's Mother, took the phone with a smile. 'Hello, Vandana, how are you, dear?'

Vandana continued, 'Aunty, I went to the doctor today, and the doctor confirmed that I'm pregnant.'

Aditya's mother's eyes sparkled with joy, and she couldn't contain her happiness. 'That's a happy news!'

As Vandana and Aditya's mother continued to share their excitement Aditya's thoughts were centered on what he saw on the field. Though the news from Vandana brought some excitement, for Aditya, the anxiety emotion because of the iron ring had become a glue-like one that attached to every other emotion. It was like excitement-anxiety, happiness-anxiety, and hunger-anxiety.

He pressed the red button on the mobile and immediately opened the calculator.

Aditya started calculating 'For ten grams, it is ten thousand rupees, for hundred grams it will be one lakh rupees. Then for one kilogram of gold, it is ten lakhs. Finally, for seventy kilos of gold, it is seven crore rupees.'

The amount of seven crore rupees added equivalent restlessness to his existing state. The last year, in 2007, Rakesh bought an acre of fertile land with good water resources for eighty thousand rupees. Proportionately, that treasure chest hidden in the field was worth seven hundred acres of land. With the treasure he discovered, he could buy the entire village.

Pulling the pillow on the shelf at his hand's distance, he rested on the cot staring at the clay-tiles roof. He was bearing seventy kilograms of weight in his head but when he equated it to seven hundred acres of land it was immense, sleepless, and restless. However, money was never in his thoughts as a priority but the revenge on the murderers of his father Raghava and the mission for which his father fought and died, rather was killed.

Aditya had carried a persistent void in his heart for countless years. When he was a mere eight years old, his father, Raghava, vanished from their lives, leaving an enduring imprint on Aditya's soul. Raghava's mysterious disappearance had left no trace of his body, with only his abandoned scooter found by the roadside. Raghava, a man without enemies or adversaries, was a beacon of kindness, a benevolent figure who touched the lives of all who knew him. He was renowned in their neighboring villages for his unwavering activism, boundless energy, and the warmth of his hospitality.

On the same day, when Aditya found the treasure, there was play in Jhagaaram by the GOST troop - Guardians of Shivan's Tale. It is this troop of wandering drama artists who keep the sacrifice of the twenty-one soldiers alive. The sacrifice of those soldiers was the reason for the treasures in the forest but other stories of propaganda backed by huge funding widely communicated those soldiers to be thieves and traitors. Only the people in the then kingdom of Vijetha Mandala were aware of the true story and surprisingly, the paid propaganda has succeeded in forwarding various theories to be discussed in that kingdom too. Even in the villages which were the birthplaces and deathbeds of many soldiers, the villages which witnessed the true story had to see the arrival of the propaganda that promoted the soldiers as traitors.

To counter the false allegations, the GOST tellers did as much as they could to tell the story interestingly and creatively every year. The summer break had always been the right season for these nomadic artists to organize stage shows. How coincidental that the same day when Aditya saw the iron ring with chain on the field, was the day the show was played.

Aditya, along with Rakesh, was present at the venue well before the troop started to set up the stage and it was dusk. Usually, such theatres are organized in vast grounds on the outskirts of the village. Aditya sat under the nearest tree to the stage. The bulged-out roots of the huge banyan tree served him the chair while Rakesh accompanied the organizers to set the stage. Holding one of the ends of the backdrop cloth, Rakesh shouted to invite Aditya but in vain. Aditya was away from the world, he was shifting his stares between the dusk-washed sky and the stage backdrop but was unaware of both scenes. Nothing made him attentive – neither the intended intricate designs of the stage curtains nor the dynamic warm hues on the sky. Both, the deliberately painted curtains by man and the unlimited hues on the huge canvas by God, both failed to captivate Aditya. As the faded shades of dusk transitioned to night, the stage blossomed into a realm of luminosity with just a few wooden planks, poles, flood lights and curtains.

At the time when the sky made it clear for the stars to appear, the audience too started appearing at the venue.

Ravidasa, the key actor and director, stood at and tested the mike to alert the audience and his troop. Aditya was keen in every detail of what was being done on the stage, even counting the twenty-one swords placed along the inner border of the stage as a symbol of reverence for the soldiers, and recognition for their sacrifice, to evoke emotions among the audience.

As a ritual, reciting the names of the twenty-one soldiers, Ravidasa started to tell the tale in the rhythm of prose and poetry.

In the realm of Vijetha Mandala fair,
A king named Yasho Mardhana ruled with no care.
With false submission to the British's might,
Mardhana forgot his own people's plight.

Let us sing their valor, let the melody rise,
For the sacrifice that touched the skies
Though their families suffered, left in despair
Their spirits live on in the songs we share.

The masters in storytelling, the enchanting weavers of words, the blenders of songs, dance, and acting started to enact the Shivan's tale. While Ravidasa was the key performer, who narrated the story from beginning to end, the other artists entered the stage as and when the story demanded them. Immediately after reciting the poem, Ravidasa slowly took the audience to the history at 1945.

With the changing backdrops aptly suited to the setting, Ravidasa started the show without missing any details in plots, settings and emotions.

An actor, dressed up heavily entered on to the stage while the background depicted a large room in a palace. The actor was playing the role of the King Raja Yasho Mardhana who was waiting to share his excitement and anxiety with his minister, Ujjwala Hari Keshava.

The submissive king and the radiant beauty

In the year 1945

'Come on in, Ujjwala. Take your seat,' the king of Vijetha Mandala kingdom invited his minister, Ujjwala Hari Keshava.

It was the minister's first time entering the king's drawing room, and he stood in awe amid the many velvet cushions and elegant carpet, unsure of where to sit.

'Why are you so lost, Ujjwala? Sit,' the king repeated. Ujjwala chose a chair near the king and gratefully sank into its plush cushions. 'Yes, my lord. Thank you,' he said, his eyes wandering between the room's aesthetics and the suspense of the king's invitation.

The king stood beside an oil lamp placed at a height, one hand on the wall, and another on his waist. The minister was not only struck by the unusual behavior of his king but also captivated by the room's opulence. Soft, warm light from oil lamps bathed the walls of the hall. The paintings on that wall primarily featured the works of Raja Ravi Varma.

The room had long arched windows draped with richly embroidered curtains. Fresh flower vases adorned each window. The crafted ceiling, the cushioned chairs, the rugged carpets, and the exquisite paintings appealed to all the minister's senses. Although he had previously observed the room from the doorway, he had never entered it, as it was reserved for the king's family and friends.

As the minister oscillated between admiration for the room's aesthetics and the suspense of the king's invitation, a servant entered, bearing a large tray with a porcelain teapot, cups, and saucers. While she served tea to both of them, the king called Ujjwala to join him near one of the paintings.

'Ujjwala, look at this painting,' the king said.

'That's truly remarkable, captivating, my lord,' replied the minister.

'Do you know about this painting, Ujjwala?' the king asked, his eyes fixed on the artwork.

'No, my king.'

'Have you heard of Raja Ravi Varma?'

'Yes, my lord.'

'This is one of his paintings. Last month, a British officer gifted it to me,' the king said proudly.

'It looks the best in the hall, my lord.'

'The painting tells the love story of Nala and Damayanthi.' Said the king.

'That's a great tale, and the painting perfectly captures the pivotal moment in their story: the celestial swan singing praises about King Nala to the charming Princess Damayanthi,' the minister interjected, eager to demonstrate his knowledge.

'Ujjwala, look at the portrait of Damayanthi here,' the king continued, his gaze never leaving the painting. 'The dark red saree with a golden zari border, the pink blouse. She is so lost in thought that she doesn't notice her pallu on the floor. She's absorbed in the words of her lover, conveyed by the mythical swan. Notice the details, Ujjwala. The thick hair, the kajal on her eyes, the bindi on her forehead.'

'I didn't notice them in such detail, my lord.'

'You've grown old, Ujjwala.'

'Perhaps, my lord.'

'Ujjwala, do you think a beauty like this exists in our kingdom?'

'No way, my lord. I don't believe such beauty exists on Earth. It resides only in the imaginations of artists, and each artist brings that imagination to life in their way.'

'But I've seen a women, more captivating than this portrait, Ujjwala.'

The minister felt a pang of annoyance at the king's words. The king, in his mid-forties, had a son in his early twenties.

'I know you are surprised to hear this from me,' the king continued, 'but I must tell you this so you can positively communicate in the kingdom.'

'As you wish, my lord. May I ask, who is she?'

'Nishitha Varshini, the princess of Maithreya Mandala.'

'Ah, I see. Her beauty is renowned in tales in our kingdom as well, my lord. It's no wonder you are captivated by her.'

'Yes, Ujjwala. I fell in love with her when I saw her at the Christmas party organized by the collector.'

'Did you express your feelings, my lord?'

'No, Ujjwala. She's only twenty-one, and I fear she may not understand my love. So, I spoke to her father, and he agreed to our marriage.'

'That's wonderful news, my lord. We shall make arrangements according to your instructions.'

As Ujjwala processed the king's revelation, he was tasked with transporting twenty-one treasure jars to Maithreya Mandala in a few days, and Jayendra Bhushana, the king's son, would provide the details.

'My lord, I would look after the transportation of the treasure but allow me to do it confidentially as the peasants are suffering from the debts and most of them have already sold the land to the money lenders.' Said Ujjwala - caught in a whirlwind of astonishment, found himself torn between the aesthetics of the magnificent room he had just admired and the weight of the king's words and revelations.

In the southernmost part of India, a small yet historically significant kingdom was inherited to Raja Vijetha Yasho Mardhana who was characterized by cowardice. Yasho Mardhana not only surrendered the sovereignty of the kingdom to the British but also displayed a submissive and servile attitude towards them. He continued to willingly enter into unequal treaty agreements, surrendering control and resources without even attempting to negotiate better terms. These agreements left his kingdom vulnerable and at the mercy of British authority.

His compliance with British orders was striking. He would execute British directives without question, regardless of whether they were unfavorable to his own people or his kingdom's interests. Whether it was imposing heavy taxes or allowing British troops to station within his territory, he did so without resistance nor at least gestured any inconvenience – in fact treated them always with great cost.

He treated the British with a lavishness that stunned observers. He showered them with gifts, hosted extravagant banquets in their honor, and provided them with luxurious accommodations, all as a testament to his unwavering loyalty and subservience to the colonial power. These gestures served as a stark reminder of his prioritization of British interests over those of his own kingdom.

The kingdom had, over time, become the default destination for British officials and guests. The ruler's lavish hosting, complete with extravagant gifts, opulent banquets, and luxurious accommodations, incurred substantial costs for the kingdom. However, the land's fertility, the impressive agricultural yield and the presence of skilled artisans ensured that these expenses did not immediately burden the kingdom, allowing this costly deference to continue for several years.

In addition to his lavish hosting, the king harbored an inexplicable ambition to amass huge gold during his lifetime, and remarkably, he had already achieved half of this audacious goal. To safeguard his wealth, he stored it in fifty treasure chests, each containing seventy kilograms of gold the form of chains, coins, bracelets and other jewelry and diamonds. The location of this immense treasure remained a closely guarded secret, known only to him and to his one and only son, Jayendra Bhushana and not a single soul in the ministry had ever laid eyes on it. Meanwhile, the kingdom's goods and finished products were regularly traded with British companies, with a substantial portion of the profits finding their way into the king's vault.

Not all days were the same, and by 1945, the kingdom had experienced three consecutive years of a severe and extended drought. This prolonged period of little to no rainfall had devastating consequences for the local farmers. They found themselves in a difficult situation where they had no choice but to sell their lands to moneylenders.

The drought had made it almost impossible for them to cultivate their fields and earn a living. With crops failing year after year, the farmers were left with no other option to sustain themselves and their families. They turned to moneylenders who, in exchange for financial relief, acquired ownership of their land.

This decision to part with their ancestral lands was not taken lightly. It was a last resort, driven by the desperation to survive in the face of a natural disaster that had left them struggling to make ends meet.

The following year brought a significant change. The heavens opened up, and heavy rainfall replenished the ponds and lakes throughout the kingdom. This much-needed rain instilled a sense of hope among the farmers.

However, for those who had sold their fertile lands during the preceding years of drought, this change in fortune was bittersweet. While they rejoiced in the prospect of better times ahead, their joy was tainted by the realization that they were no longer part of this revival. Their once-productive lands, now in the hands of moneylenders, were beyond their reach.

The contrasting emotions of hope and regret painted a complex picture of the kingdom's agricultural recovery, with some celebrating the return of prosperity, while others mourned their lost opportunities. A lot of people in the kingdom were hoping that the king would use his huge treasure to help them out of their difficulties. But as they soon discovered, this dream was just too far-fetched. The king's enormous wealth was a well-kept secret, hidden away and impossible for the common people to access. So, their expectations of getting help from the king were shattered, and they had to face the harsh truth of their situation all on their own.

On the other hand, in the grand meeting hall known as the Darbar, the king proudly declared his ambition to accumulate a hundred chests of gold, leaving his councilors in a state of helplessness. They dared not challenge the king, for their positions were crucial.

'Your goal is just a few chests away, my lord, and in three years, you'll surely achieve this dream, the rains too are in favor this year.' a loyal councilor said, attempting to uplift the king's spirits.

Such Darbars were attended by four councilors and their secretaries, a chief councilor, the army chief, and five personal advisors to the king and the minister.

'But, may we inquire about your plans for this gold, my lord? Your strategies have always been surprising,' another councilor, with a touch of wit, asked.

'I sense your curiosity, councilor, but you're correct, it will remain a surprise,' the king replied.

Conversations continued until the king inquired about the rumors in the kingdom.

Rishabha Kumara, the Army Chief, sitting alongside the councilors, nudged his counterpart, the chief councilor to remind him of the issue they wanted to discuss in the Darbar.

'My lord, it concerns the moneylenders tormenting the peasants.' The chief councilor responded promptly to the nudge.

'The peasants possess land, and the lenders have money. Let them trade. Increased trade leads to economic progress,' an advisor to the king interjected, encouraged by the king's smile.

'Apologies, my lord, but peasants have only land, while the moneylenders, in addition to money, are now accumulating land as well,' the chief communicated humbly, with a touch of humor.

'Yes, my lord, a few peasants have become daily laborers in their own fields. If this trend continues, it will create economic imbalance for generations, irreversibly,' supported another councilor, prompting the king to respond.

'Provide a solution that doesn't involve penalizing the moneylenders or depleting our reserves. Remember, as per British law, moneylending is legal, and we cannot go against it,' the king stood up, and everyone followed suit.

'Nature takes care of us; let's wait and see. Meanwhile, I order the chief priest to organize rituals for everyone's well-being.' The king was almost concluding when he suddenly spoke again.

'But for sure you and the entire kingdom has an exciting news which our minister shares with you now and I leave for the day.' Said the king and left the Darbar.

The Darbar stood up as a respect while the king left and started to walk to the minister out of curiosity.

'What else are you planning this time Ujjwala? Any peanuts distribution for the peasants?' Joked the chief councilor.

'No, you will be shocked, literally shocked if I shared the exciting news and by the way the news is exciting for the king and not for you or me, ok.' Said Ujjwala.

'Ok, tell us the news.' Everyone pleaded to complete the formality so that they could leave the palace.

'The princess of Maithreya mandala, Nishitha Varshini, is going to be the queen of this Vijetha mandala.' Revealed the minister but didn't realize the mistake he did in communicating it.

'Ooh, the Prince, Jayendra is getting married?' said a counselor and the minister tried to correct but other councilors too started to add their voice for which Ujjwala had to raise his voice to be heard.

'It is the king who is going to marry the princess of Maithreya Mandala, Nishitha Varshini.' All the voices stopped at this statement.

'But why?' asked Rishabha Kumara, the army chief.

'He is in love with her, it seems, and that she is the most beautiful one on the earth for our king.' The minister added.

'Did she agree?' Enquired one there.

'Yes.'

'But how come. I also heard that she is very beautiful but how can she marry someone who is double her age?'

'Because, we are giving twenty one treasure jars away to her father in return' said the minister and urged them 'When we go out to the people, just say that the king has made us proud by marrying the most beautiful women on the earth. It's the pride of our kingdom.'

'Ooh, you can turn anything to positive, that's why you are chosen to be the minister.' Someone in the group joked.

After the Darbar had concluded, the completely informal conversations began outside the palace among the advisors and councilors. Under a huge banyan tree, all of the Darbar members sat on the bulged roots of the tree and shared their thoughts randomly.

'Do you grasp the gravity of this, Rishabha? Nearly every peasant in some villages of our kingdom has lost a piece of land to the moneylenders,' the Chief councilor remarked looking at Rishabha Kumara.

Rishabha belonged to the community of Shivanas, a community deeply entrenched in a tradition of military service. Shivana's had a long history of dedicating themselves to the armed forces of Vijetha Mandala. For generations, the Shivana's clan had remained steadfast in their commitment to defending the kingdom.

However, a significant shift occurred when King Yasho Mardhana ascended the throne. With a perceived reduction in external threats and a growing alliance with the British, the King began to discourage the recruitment of more soldiers into the army. However, this new stance conflicted with the deeply ingrained desire of the Shivanas community, who overwhelmingly aspired to serve in the army. The subjects thought that their king Yasho Mardhana was a clever diplomat, as he could not fight the mighty empire of British, it is better to garner their respect. That their king's actions were driven to avoid conflict that lead to maintaining the dignity and independence of their kingdom.

'Look, we've known the king for decades. He does as he pleases. You and I were appointed to show the British that our kingdom has a functioning administrative structure,' one of the advisors to the king intervened.

'Anyone who tries to enlighten the king ends up replaced; it's as simple as that,' chimed in another advisor.

'Do you all know what's more are the king's gifts to Maithreya Mandala?' the Minister asked, drawing everyone closer in curiosity.

Pausing to observe the intrigued faces around him, he revealed the secret, 'Twenty-one villages to govern, twenty-one chests of gold, twenty-one pairs of horses, a golden palanquin weighing twenty-one kilograms adorned with diamonds. And you may be wondering why 21? It is the age of the princess.'

'Thank God, the princess is not fifty years old, had it been so, then the entire kingdom, including you and me would have been sold.' Rishabha released some satires while others busted into laughter and Rishabha quickly transformed his thoughts serious and continued, 'Chief, just this palanquin could clear half of the peasants' debts. It's disheartening; are we here merely to witness the spectacle?' expressed Rishabha, his voice tinged with frustration.

'Rishabha, you seem too idealistic to comprehend a king's ways. You need to grow up. Do you think our kingdom needs an army? How many Shivanas fought for the kingdom? You are sent to serve and fight for the British. Shivanas are meant to sacrifice for the Vijetha Mandala but you are sacrificing for the British, you are on the enemy's side. This is our fate.' Said the Chief and continued, 'Shall I reveal something that will further trouble you?' When the Chief advisor said this, the onlookers mentally prepared themselves for more revelations, expecting numerous properties in sets of twenty-one. However, they were utterly shocked when he disclosed, 'The moneylenders' association has secured a contract from the king to provide lunch in every village on the day of the princess's wedding and distribute clothes throughout the kingdom.'

'The king is favoring the wealthy even more. There's no justice here. What if someone reports this to the British government and it's pathetic that the people live a cowardly life, they have to revolt?' Rishabha's words seem too innocent but they are rebellious.

'It's better we end this discussion here. Sometimes, we must recognize the limits of our influence and capability. The British government officials will be the chief guests at the wedding. Their stay here, along with the lavish entertainment they'll receive, will make them deaf to any complaints against the king.'

The Chief advisor did everything in his power to convey that there was no solution to the peasants' problems and that convincing the king was an impossible task but among the group, it was Rishabha who seemed comparatively concerned and exhibited subtle rebellious attitude.

In just a single day, the news of the King's marriage circulated the entire kingdom in a manner that made the kingdom feel proud of the king initially for a day or two. But later, the logic emerged among the masses on the return gifts to Maithreya mandala insulted them.

While the ministers and the subjects in the kingdom were utterly disappointed with the gesture of their king, jealousy tugged at the prince Jayendra's, heart. He couldn't shake the unease that enveloped him when he considered the extravagant gifts earmarked for the wedding. He was going to be the future king and was worried about so much loss of wealth to another kingdom and was more worried about what more would his father give away to the most beautiful women after the marriage.

The neighboring rulers to Vijetha Mandala were always fancied by the extravagantness of the king Raja Yasho Mardhana and his extrovert nature in impressing the British, he acted like a bridge between the British and the Kings. The ruler of Maithreya kingdom agreed for the marriage because of two reasons – one is the offer of the gifts and the other was that anytime if he or his sons needed some help from the British, Raja Yasho Mardhana would be there for them. The ruler of Maithreya Mandala had amassed wealth not more than ten percent of what Raja Yasho Mardhana had and hence could not say no to such a huge offer. Fortunately, the princess too was obedient to her family.

As the clear successor to the throne, the prince Jayendra found himself flooded with disappointment as he witnessed the grand preparations. He desperately wished to restrain the excessive spending, but circumstances left him feeling entirely powerless. Days passed, and despite his earnest intentions, he found no opportunity to voice his concerns.

As promised, the twenty-one villages were formally integrated into the neighboring kingdom and all other promise too were kept and the only gift left was to transport twenty-one treasure jars which had to be done the day after the wedding as agreed upon by both parties.

Amidst the bustling preparations for the wedding, the prince Jayendra, on a morning, sought a secret meeting with Rishabha, a week before. He had to express his deep concerns about losing the twenty-one treasure chests to the neighboring kingdom. However, he couldn't reveal his true intentions, so he decided to craft a clever ploy.

'Rishabha, I need your help,' the prince began. Rishabha, loyal and ever at the ready, responded, 'Yes, Prince, at your command.'

'I need your advice, Rishabha,' the prince continued, maintaining a facade of concern.

Rishabha, slightly surprised by the prince's request for counsel, remarked with a hint of humor, 'A prince seeking advice from a soldier!'

The prince, his true intentions carefully masked, said earnestly, 'Yes, Rishabha, tell me what's happening in the kingdom.'

Rishabha, sensing the gravity of the situation but not the prince's hidden agenda, responded, 'It's all about the buzz surrounding the king's marriage, dear prince. What else could be of greater importance?'

The prince, trying to maintain his pretense, replied, 'You needn't be so polite, Rishabha. I'm not a child. Everyone is comparing the extravagant wedding gifts to Maithreya kingdom with the burdens of the peasants.'

Rishabha, still not fully grasping the prince's intentions, nodded solemnly. 'Unfortunately, that's true, prince. I share your concerns. Also glad to know you too feel same like us.'

'As a prince and as a son, I find it all quite senseless, so much loss for many peasants for last three years and the very few money lenders gained. Why this treasure can't be spent for the peasants?' the prince continued, 'and it's baffling that the people don't seem to oppose and that makes me angrier, they can't be so obedient.'

Rishabha, unmindful of the prince's true motives, replied, 'Yes, prince, they are indeed innocent, obedient, and often driven by fear.'

'I want to address this issue of the peasants' debts,' the prince declared, his intentions hidden behind a veil of fake concern, 'but it may require a sacrifice from you.'

Rishabha, always loyal, responded without hesitation, 'Always for you, prince,' unaware of the hidden agenda concealed beneath the prince's words.

'I've got some plans and shall let you know them this evening. But, make sure that all our meetings are in secrecy. I shall inform you after dinner time.' They dispersed and the prince succeeded in making Rishabha believe that the he was worried about the peasants.

As the sun dipped below the horizon, casting long shadows across the palace grounds, the prince secretly summoned Rishabha. A sense of urgency weighed heavily in the air, and the prince and his childhood friend and cousin, Hikkira, had chosen an isolated spot deep within the palace gardens, shrouded by trees and overgrown vines.

Rishabha, ever faithful to the prince's summons, arrived, his curiosity to listen to the prince's plan to safeguard the treasure had dancing in him since morning. He found the prince, standing in the dappled moonlight, a somber expression on his face and Hikkira stood beside the prince with his head bent low in disappointment.

'Rishabha,' Hikkira began, 'The prince has called you here for a matter of utmost importance.'

Rishabha nodded, his unwavering loyalty mirrored in his steady gaze. 'I'm at your service, Sir.'

Hikkira's voice dropped to a hushed tone, carrying an air of secrecy. 'The Prince has been entrusted with a grave responsibility, Rishabha. The task of transporting the treasure.'

Rishabha was listening keenly and the prince chimed in a little louder voice 'But I cannot do it, I feel ashamed to be a part of this, rather I slit my throat.'

Understanding the prince's concern, Rishabha leaned in attentively, his loyalty unwavering. 'What do you propose, prince?'

Hikkira nodded, a grim determination etched on his face. 'Rishabha, the minister Ujjwala suggested that it wouldn't be wise to take the treasure through the villages as part of the procession. The subjects feel humiliated at such a huge transfer of the kingdom's wealth, he opined.'

'Of course, sir, that is for sure, they feel humiliated.' Confirmed Rishabha.

Hikkira took the lead to unfold a well-conceived strategy and said 'Look Rishabha, we have devised a plan that would safeguard the treasure and then to be used by the peasants who lost their land but it needs meticulous plan and coordination and we felt, only you can do it.' This made Rishabha to feel proud of his capability and that the identity he had in the mind of the prince.

'We need you to gather twenty of our most trustworthy soldiers, Rishabha, those who will follow your lead without a question.' Said Hikkira.

Rishabha nodded in acknowledgment of understanding the intentions of the prince. Honored by the trust placed in him, he replied 'I shall do as you ask, prince.'

Hikkira continued, 'Once you have the men ready, I'll approach the king and convince the King that it would be more fitting to transport the treasure through the forest. I shall explain that it doesn't befit our kingdom to parade such opulence through the struggling villages. The king will likely agree.'

Rishabha understood the gravity of the task. 'I am sure if you and the minister Ujjwala says, he would not have a second thought.'

The prince stood silently and let the conversation happen. 'Once we have the king's approval, you shall lead the convoy through the forest, but there, Rishabha, you must deviate from the path. Deep within the forest lies the caves of Rishi Pahar Mountain. It is there that we hide the treasure, ensuring it remains concealed.' The actual plan was exposed by Hikkira while the prince stood in the approval for the plan.

Your Highness, what shall we do after we've hidden the treasure? Won't the king become suspicious when he hears that the treasure has not been delivered as planned?'

The prince, his face veiled in shadows, leaned forward, his eyes glittering with a hidden agenda. 'Rishabha, you raise valid concerns. We must be cautious. The neighboring kingdom is known to have many dacoits and enemies. We shall exploit this to our advantage, making it appear as though they are responsible for the disappearance of the treasure. Their name and blame shall rest squarely upon them.'

Rishabha confirmed the plan and said 'And it works, prince, as this transport begins the immediate day after the marriage, the new queen would be the witness to the beginning of our journey to the forest.'

Hikkira nodded in apparent agreement and said, 'Prince, but we must also think of Rishabha and his soldiers. How will they fare once the treasure is hidden?'

The prince, a sly smile concealed in the shadows, continued, 'Rishabha, we are deeply concerned about your well-being. You and your soldiers will be deep within the forest with a valuable treasure, and we cannot bear the thought of any harm befalling you.'

Hikkira chimed in, his words laced with a hidden agenda, 'Indeed, we must ensure your safety, Rishabha, and that of your loyal men. It's essential for the success of this mission. We shall take care of you.'

The prince added 'Rishabha, once you've hidden the treasure deep within the caves of Rishi Pahar Mountain, I shall send

Hikkira the next day. He will be in disguise, appearing as though he was searching for you. In reality, he will bring with you an ample supply of food and provisions that should sustain you for few days.'

Rishabha, sensing the concern of his prince and his friend, felt a surge of gratitude. 'Thank you, Your Highness, and Hikkira, for your genuine concern. I am committed to the mission, but I appreciate your thoughts for our well-being.'

The prince nodded, his eyes revealing a sparkle of deceit that Rishabha couldn't detect. 'Rishabha, rest assured, we have a plan in place to ensure your safety and the safekeeping of the treasure. We won't let any harm come to you and by the time you return from the forest, we shall ensure that the King would sympathize with you. And later we shall plan on how to monetize the treasure and share it among the peasants.'

Rishabha, touched by their apparent concern, finally relented. 'I appreciate your thoughtfulness, Your Highness, Prince and Hikkira sir. With your plan and protection, I am ready to see this mission through.'

The prince and Hikkira exchanged a knowing glance, their hidden intentions carefully concealed. They had successfully convinced Rishabha to accept the plan, unaware of the dark fate that awaited the loyal soldiers in the depths of the forest.

'And something more important, Rishabha,' the prince spoke in a stressing tone.

'Do keep on writing the names of the peasants who suffered the most as per your knowledge or whenever you come across but do not directly enquire. Ok.' Said the prince to communicate the intentions that were absent.

The actual scheme had been carefully thought out by the prince, his clever friend, Hikkira and surprisingly the minister Ujjwala, with the goal of deceiving and eventually removing Rishabha and his loyal soldiers from the equation. However, this dark plan had been in motion for a longer period than anyone suspected but intentionally revealed to Rishabha a week before so that there was less time to think logically.

The scheme was conceived a month before the grand wedding when the Prince, the minister Ujjwala and Hikkira had gathered in the privacy of their chambers to create their wicked plan. This plan not only aimed to steal the treasure but also involved framing Rishabha, the unsuspecting and dedicated soldier. Rishabha was suggested by Ujjwala as he had been observing the rebellious attitude, more emotional nature mixed with a little of innocence. Time was of the essence, so they had intentionally provoked Rishabha into action just a week days before the wedding, leaving him with no time to doubt or rethink his commitment, he only would spend time in motivating twenty more soldiers for the mission.

However, the true intent of the scheme was decidedly more nefarious. The prince and his confidant, Hikkira, planned to travel with the soldiers until they reached the halfway point. At the junction where the path veered towards the Rishi Pahar Mountain, the treacherous duo intended to serve a poisoned meal—a malevolent blend designed to ensure the gradual and agonizing demise of Rishabha and his unsuspecting comrades. The poison they possessed was of a foreign origin, a substance Hikkira had somehow managed to procure. Its sinister trait lay in its slow-acting nature, manifesting its effects only after a considerable delay of ten to fourteen hours.

Once the soldiers had succumbed to the poison, their deaths would be attributed to the imaginary bandits who had allegedly abducted them and stolen the treasure. The blame, neatly placed on these shadowy foes, would divert suspicion away from the true culprits - the prince, the minister and Hikkira.

The further plan was - with the soldiers out of the picture, the treasure would remain concealed in the harsh terrain of the Rishi Pahar Mountains. The prince and Hikkira would wait patiently for the right moment to retrieve the treasure and relocate it to a more convenient and secure place, cementing their wicked plans and leaving no evidence of their dark actions.

As the clock counted down to the significant day of the grand wedding, Rishabha and his loyal soldiers remained blissfully unaware of the sinister trap that awaited them. The palace buzzed with excitement and anticipation, all the while hiding the deceitful drama of betrayal and treachery that was set to unfold beneath the veneer of celebration.

Following tradition, the king, accompanied by his family and friends, journeyed to the Maithreya Mandala to unite in matrimony with the princess. The king and Nishitha Varshini, the newly-wedded queen of Vijetha Mandala then made their way back in a grand procession of horse carts until they reached the entrance of the Vijetha Mandala fort. Here, a significant transition took place – from the horse carts, the couple would now be transported on a palanquin, a few hundred meters from the fort.

A spacious palanquin, designed for the comfort of the new couple, awaited them. The responsibility of bearing this royal palanquin fell upon the strong shoulders of the Shivans' team. With grace and precision, the majestic palanquin, held aloft by eight bearers – four at the front and four at the back – made its regal progress towards the Vijetha Mandala fortress. The palanquin was draped with transparent cloth adorned with intricate folded designs on two sides, offering spectators a teasingly blurred glimpse of the royal couple within. The fort was buzzing with a massive gathering, not solely there to shower blessings upon the newlyweds, but predominantly to catch a glimpse of the most beautiful woman on Earth, Nishitha Varshini.

However, much to the disappointment of the onlookers, the transparent cloth veiling the palanquin rendered only fleeting views of the captivating face within. The lanterns carried by the attendants illuminated the palanquin, making it a spectacle in itself, but could not penetrate the curtains of the palanquin, once in a while, for a minute, the king unfurled the curtains to wave at the crowd and show his new wife. Adorned with flowers and accompanied by the melody of musical bands and rhythmic hymns, the palanquin progressed ceremoniously toward the fort's entrance.

The palanquin bearers felt proud of the opportunity to carry the king and the queen. It wasn't a burden for them, indeed a pleasure to boast for life. Along the way of the palanquin were there many crests and troughs, but the bearers ensured no jerks in that journey.

As it traversed from the fort's entrance to its inner sanctum, only a select few remained in attendance when the palanquin was gently placed on the ground within the temple boundaries inside the fort. The assembly till the temple included the eight dedicated palanquin bearers, the king's son Jayendra, ministers, priests, advisors, Hikkira, and a handful of close relatives. All eyes, however, were fervently fixed on the quest to catch a glimpse of the new queen.

With her right foot first on the ground, the queen, Nishitha Varshini got out from the palanquin, only to enter into another bigger palanquin, the fort. As the practice, the king and the new queen had to offer prayers at the temple inside and break a coconut each as an offer to God.

For every spectator there, it was not at all a sight of the couple, it was just the presence of Nishitha Varshini, the name that was most discussed across the kingdom for the beauty that was associated with it. As the king Yasho Mardhana and the queen Nishitha Varshini started to walk to the temple, the king went unnoticed. Had there been a laser light for the eyes of the spectators, not even one would had a spot on the king, he was neglected, neglected so much that he was almost absent in the scene. And those happenings were worthy and the queen deserved even more, she deserved earthly attention, sorry, she deserved cosmic attention.

Draped in a red silk saree, filled with peacock designs across the pallu with a dark shiny blue border, she walked like a lioness with her head and eyes straight and forward. Along her way from the entrance of the temple to the sanctum, there were many sculptures of beautiful women which were claimed to be the most precise work by the most acclaimed sculptors. Had those sculptures around had any sense, they would have hidden in shame if not broken into pieces, realizing they were not worthy to be called beautiful in the presence of Nishitha Varshini. As she reached the idol in the temple and started to offer the prayers, the priests too wondered at her, they realized that a closer glance at her in itself was a blessing for their entire service at the temple - of course, as they claim, the priests usually have the opportunity to meet and talk to divine beings – now they can support that claim to have seen an angel closely.

Her face was just right, not big, not small, like an autumn full moon, embedded the features with zero errors in symmetry and precision. The golden skin, tight and plum, reflected the lanterns light, brighter than the lanterns. She defied the principles of light the secondary source of light cannot be brighter than its primary source - she amplified the light. Her eyebrows resembled the sexiest curve a wild eagle could make while taking its highest flight towards a prey in the sky. Her eyes like the butterfly nebula, were a proof of the unity of the cosmos, and the relationship between humanity and the broader universe.

The lips were carved like a bow arrowing at the sky with its string pulled a little and the colour of her lips was an eternal confusion as they stood at the juncture of hues between red and pink. The most fascinating feature was her nose. It was so perfect that if an alien should be taught what a human being's nose looks like, one would use hers. The most precious diamonds and the intricate designs of the jewelry she wore felt insulted as they went unnoticed on her neck and ears.

Imagine, Lord Bramha holding the laser-sharp chisel and had been sweating to round the earlobe of Nishitha Varshini! Such was the flawlessness in her beauty. That is why in the God's court, if the common man complained that the king was gifting the kingdom's wealth to Nishitha Varshini, God would support the king, for He knows, the deal was still a peanut to own her.

Had she appeared as a moon, the circadian rhythm would have reversed for the only reason that men would just spend time watching the moon and then continue to sleep during the day. Had she been a flower and the rocks had known her, then they would weather in just a second to bear the plant that grows those flowers – weathering is a process of soil formation from rocks that takes millions of years.

After the prayer at the temple, the couple waved their hands and walked onto the staircase to walk further towards the living area. No man who saw the queen close would have slept that night, had anyone slept, he was not a man!

But for the palanquin bearers, the next fateful day had finally dawned and the treasure chests too had.

The Sinister Scheme and the Sacrifice

The treasure chest, an exquisite work of art, stood in splendid isolation in the backyard of the huge fort. Made entirely of polished brass, it took the shape of a unique jar, with a distinct cylindrical form that captured the eye. Every detail of this magnificent container made the witnesses of it broaden the images and amounts of treasure inside it.

The cap, which securely sealed the jar's contents, was fitted with meticulously designed screws. Each screw was perfectly aligned, allowing the cap to be fastened tightly, guarding the treasure within from the prying eyes of the world.

From the neck of the cylindrical chest dangled a long and robust iron chain, an unadorned contrast to the golden hue of the brass. At the end of this iron chain hung an impressive iron ring, a circle of considerable proportions, measuring about half a foot in diameter. Its size suggested the weight and importance of the chest's cargo. But what truly set this treasure chest apart was its intricate design - The entire surface, from the bottom to the cap, the chain, and the massive iron ring, was adorned with embossed designs. These designs showcased the kingdom's unparalleled craftsmanship. Each design, painstakingly etched, added to the overall grandeur of the brass jar – the jar itself was a treasure.

The iron chain, an integral part of the treasure chest's design, served a crucial purpose beyond mere aesthetics. It was a thoughtful innovation carefully planned by the king to ensure that the chest could be moved by even an individual of relatively low physical strength. This feature was not just a matter of convenience; it was a deliberate strategy to safeguard the treasure even in the absence of support from any friend or family member – he believed treasure can make anyone go to any extent.

The king understood the inherent vulnerability of having such a valuable cache of riches. The treasure was of immeasurable worth, and the king couldn't simply entrust its transportation to others, no matter how trusted they may be. This sense of insecurity led to the ingenious design of the chest, with the iron chain and ring playing pivotal roles.

Yasho Mardhana dedicated extensive time and meticulous planning to safeguard the treasure and not a fraction of that effort was devoted to the kingdom's well-being.

The prince and Hikkira convinced Yasho Mardhana that they would accompany the soldiers on horse-drawn carts till halfway until they reached a place where the path became too narrow and rough for any horse-drawn carts to go through. After that point, the soldiers knew they'd have to carry the treasure themselves.

The soldiers loaded the treasure chests into the three carts. In addition to securing the chests, they ingeniously arranged themselves to make efficient use of the available space. In each cart, seven soldiers seated, skillfully positioning their bodies to accommodate both the chests and themselves.

With the chests and soldiers securely arranged, the convoy was now ready to continue its journey deeper into the forest - the carefully orchestrated plan was set into motion. Twenty-one loyal soldiers, along with the Prince and his confidant,

Hikkira, embarked on their journey toward the neighboring kingdom.

With every step taking them closer to their destination, the tension in the air was tangible. The soldiers, their loyalty unwavering, continued their march under the watchful eyes of their beloved prince.

As the day's journey brought them to a designated stop to reroute towards the Rishi Pahar Mountain, the group settled down for a seemingly innocent lunch break. It was at this critical juncture that Hikkira, the architect of the evil scheme, sprang into action. With practiced precision, he carefully served the poisoned food to the unsuspecting soldiers.

However, in a devious twist to their plan, Hikkira ensured that both he and the prince served themselves from dishes that had not been tainted with the deadly substance. As the midday sun hung high in the sky, the group had finished their ill-omened meal, unaware of the sinister fate that lurked beneath the surface.

But just as they were about to disperse, one of the soldiers spoke up. His voice, though filled with determination, carried a hint of uncertainty as he addressed the prince and Hikkira. 'Your Highness, Hikkira sir, would you mind if I packed some food in this banana leaf? I find myself unable to consume a full lunch, and I shall have some more along the way.'

'Do you need the permission, soldier, you are free to serve yourselves.' The prince intertwined and offered the banana leaf.

The soldier felt great that the prince himself spoke to him and offered the banana leaf, and he continued to pack the leftover food.

Minutes later to lunch, to prepare to start to the destination, the soldiers gathered in an orderly formation, their faces turned toward the prince and Hikkira. Rishabha, their steadfast leader, stood at the forefront. The prince stepped forward, his expression a mix of determination and gratitude, as he addressed his loyal comrades.

'I want to express my deepest gratitude to every one of you. Today's task is of great importance to our kingdom, and I have complete faith in your abilities. In the caves that lay at the starting of the Rishi Pahar Mountain, you would find a painted entrance, you must dig a pit that's at least six feet deep, secure the treasure chest within it by winding the long chain around it.'

I want my friend Hikkira to share his words as you venture into the risky task.

'Dear comrades, not every life is blessed to have a purpose but ours is such. When we thought of this plan to safeguard our kingdom's wealth, I was not sure that we would find people like you so quick. All credit goes to Rishabha. I don't know if anyone of you read English poems. I want to recite you of a poem by Henry Wadsworth Longfellow, an influential English poet.

In the world's broad field of battle,
In the bivouac of Life,
Be not like dumb, driven cattle!
Be a hero in the strife!

I always longed to see those real heroes in the strife and this moment I am standing here in front of them. This is my life time opportunity to meet you, my heroes. As we part now, I want to hear a few words from anyone of you.'

The youngest of the soldier raised his hand.

'Sir, we had two routes to transport the treasure. One is along the main road, crossing the villages in the kingdom, and the other one is this forest route, and we have chosen the toughest one. I too remembered the poem by my favorite poet, Robert Frost,

"I shall be telling this with a sigh
Somewhere ages and ages hence:
Two roads diverged in a wood, and I—
I took the one less traveled by,
And that has made all the difference."'

'Impressed, young soldier, we are impressed. I am sure you had been to the finest schools.' Replied Hikkira.

'No Sir, my father taught me everything.'

'Ooh, very great of him. So soldiers, march on to become the heroes in the strife.' The prince intervened to cut the conversation as it was getting late.

After those words, the prince carefully placed the weighty brass jar onto their shoulders. Each soldier bore this precious cargo with a sense of honor and responsibility. On their backs, they carried leather bags, inside of which lay the essential tools for the task ahead - a digging rod and a shovel.

The prince's instructions were delivered with clarity, leaving no room for doubt. As they absorbed his words, a collective sense of purpose enveloped the group. They were a team, bound by their loyalty to the prince and their kingdom.

With that, the group resumed their journey, each person lost in their thoughts and conversations, while the Prince and his friend returned to the kingdom in the horse carts. Unknown to the soldiers, the slow-acting poison had begun its subtle and deadly work. The die had been cast, and the wheels of their wicked fate were set in motion.

The soldiers pressed on, their determined footsteps echoing through the dense forest as they continued their journey. They had walked for a solid two hours, with brief pauses to rest and catch their breath. The anticipation of reaching their destination, coupled with their sense of duty, kept them moving steadily forward.

They were not more than a kilometer away from the mountain, and a sense of eagerness and happiness filled their hearts. However, as they pressed on, one of the soldiers began to falter. He expressed a desire to sit down, citing feelings of difficulty walking and general unease. His experience resonated with two others in the group, who also found the journey increasingly challenging.

Seeking respite, they veered toward a nearby water stream, the soothing sound of flowing water offering a momentary solace. The soldiers found sturdy rocks to sit upon, hoping to regain their strength - Amidst this brief interval, the situation took a sudden and alarming turn.

Out of nowhere, one of the soldiers began to vomit uncontrollably, collapsing to the ground in distress. Rishabha, quick to respond, fetched water and carefully administered it to the afflicted soldier. After a brief rest, the soldier, although fatigued, expressed his readiness to continue.

However, their respite was short-lived, as another soldier voiced similar discomfort, describing a sensation of heaviness that weighed upon him. Concern rippled through the group as it became apparent that something was seriously amiss.

Rishabha, demonstrating leadership and compassion, recommended that everyone take a few minutes to rest and recharge, hoping that a brief pause would provide the energy needed to continue their journey.

But then, one of the soldiers, who had packed the provisions during lunch, decided it was time for him for a quick meal to replenish his energy. He opened the bundled banana leaf, only to be met with an unsettling sight and an even more distressing smell. The food had an unusual odor, and the color had shifted, taking on an unappetizing hue.

Concerned, the soldier held up the tainted meal for his comrades to see and shouted 'We are poisoned, we are poisoned'. After looking at the food, a wave of unease washed over the group as they collectively realized that something was terribly amiss. The soldiers were aware of how to notice food that was poisoned. It spoils quickly, becomes watery, decomposes and changes its color to light brown and smells rotten. Their initial shock was swiftly replaced by a chilling awareness: they had been poisoned.

Fear and confusion spread among the soldiers. They exchanged alarmed glances, their hearts heavy with dread as they comprehended the gravity of the situation. The trust they had placed in the provisions had been betrayed, and the consequences were horrible.

In this remote corner of the forest, far from any help, the soldiers now faced an agonizing dilemma. As the reality of their poisoned meal sank in, they knew that they would need to act swiftly to confront this treacherous threat and find a way to survive.

The soldiers' thoughts drifted to the families they had left behind. Each soldier carried with them the treasured memories of their loved ones - the loving embrace of their spouse, the laughter of their children, and the wisdom of their parents.

Tears welled up in their eyes. Some soldiers, unable to contain their emotions, allowed tears to stream down their cheeks.

Meanwhile, some in the group instinctively recognized the need for solidarity and emotional support. They came together, forming small circles of mutual comfort. Soldiers embraced one another, their silent hugs offering solace in this shared moment of despair. These embraces conveyed a profound understanding of the emotional anguish they all faced. In this remote corner of the forest, amidst the sounds of their comrades' sobs and the gentle rustling of leaves, the soldiers found solace in their shared humanity. They were warriors, yes, but they were also fathers, sons, and brothers. In their vulnerability and unity, they reaffirmed their unwavering commitment to the mission.

Only Rishabha stood far as guilt weighed heavily on his heart. It had been he who had convinced and motivated his fellow soldiers for this crucial mission, firmly believing in the prince's words without a trace of doubt. But now, as the poison began its insidious work, Rishabha found himself overwhelmed by regret.

'I can't believe I led you into this. I trusted the prince, and now...' Rishabha's voice trembled as tears streamed down his face. His comrades, despite their discomfort, gathered around him, their expressions reflecting genuine concern and empathy.

'It's not your fault, Rishabha. None of us saw this coming. We all believed in the prince,' reassured one soldier.

'Exactly. He played us all, and we fell for it,' remarked another soldier.

Rishabha, his voice quivering with guilt and regret, implored his comrades for forgiveness. 'Please, my friends, find it in your hearts to forgive me. I never wanted any of this to happen.'

Even as they dealt with their suffering and the ugly betrayal they faced in the mission, the soldiers offered Rishabha solace and understanding. As they gathered around, Rishabha, their leader, initiated the discussion.

Rishabha's voice quivered as he began, 'Shivanas, my dear friends, it's clear now that we've been poisoned. Our time is slipping away, and we must face the harsh truth that survival may not be in the cards for us. But remember this: our mission cannot fail. We won't allow the prince to enjoy the spoils of this deceitful act. Let's discuss how we can safeguard these chests, even in our final moments.'

The soldiers nodded solemnly and one among them added, 'Rishabha is right. Our duty to our kingdom doesn't waver, even as our time grows short. Let's put our heads together, and figure out a way to hide these chests so that no one can lay claim to them.'

Firmly, another soldier chimed in, 'Agreed. We may not have much time left, but we'll make every moment count. The prince won't have the satisfaction and the treasure should reach our people. '

In this shadowed enclave of the forest, their voices carried the weight of determination.

One soldier furrowed his brow in thought and suggested, 'What if we move the treasure to another distant mountain?'

Another soldier, concern etched across his face, responded, 'True, but the journey would be dangerous, and time is not on our side.'

A third soldier contemplated, 'What about the nearby village, Jhagaram? We could give the treasure to the villagers, but it's not without risks. Word might spread, and the king could find out.'

A fourth soldier interjected, 'Maybe we should think about other options. Giving the treasure randomly is not wise.'

A fifth soldier, showing healthy skepticism, voiced his concerns, 'Money lenders? But they're known for their greed. I'm not sure we can trust them.'

Rishabha said, 'I am angry on everyone in the kingdom, neither the king has any self-respect, nor do we have the strength to educate the king and the subjects have no dare to question or revolt. I don't want to give the treasure as a gift but it should be hard earned, it should be fought for even if it is not got, they will learn to fight and earn.'

Then came a sixth soldier, a young and creative member of their group, who offered a glimmer of hope, 'What if we hide the treasure in a complex pattern in the forest? We could create a detailed code that would be incredibly hard to decipher. Even if someone manages to crack it, finding the treasure would still be a tough challenge.'

The group collectively breathed a sigh of relief, their faces reflecting a renewed sense of determination. In their darkest hour, this plan presented a ray of hope—a chance to protect the treasure chests and more than the plan, the confidence in the youngster's words was like a well-aimed sword strike.

'Sounds great, but do we know how much time we have to breathe here to develop the pattern and code.' Asked a soldier.

'Sounds great, but do we know how much time we have to breathe here?' asked a soldier.

'It's a slow poison we are exposed to; it would take nearly twelve to fifteen more hours to kill us – a very rarely available poison,' educated the young soldier.

'Hey, young soldier, I have never heard of a poison that acts so slowly with a single dose,' inquired Rishibha.

'Did you notice the prince's friend Hikkira? The handle of his sword has an embossed komodo dragon symbol,' said the young soldier.

'Yes, we did,' came the chorus from the soldiers.

'Komodo dragon's saliva is a slow poison. Usually, the Komodo dragon bites its prey and follows the prey wherever it goes. After waiting until its prey falls sick or dies, the komodo eats it. The poison we are ingested with is made using that saliva. The poison acts by thinning the blood gradually.' The young soldier educated

Rishabha leaned in, his voice carrying a sense of urgency, 'So fatal. The treasure must remain concealed, and it should be a hard-earned secret. Can you come up with a code, young one?'

The youthful soldier nodded resolutely. 'Just give me a few moments,' he replied. Stepping away from the group, he ventured a few places towards the looming Rishi Pahar Mountain. His eyes scanned the surroundings, taking in the towering trees and the lush vegetation.

Returning to his comrades, the young soldier beckoned them closer. 'Gather around, everyone, and walk with me' he called, motioning them to join him.

After a few meters walk, he halted and said 'You see, where we're standing now, we are aligned with the Shiva temple. Can you see the temple straight on the mountain?' asked the young soldier.

The distance from our current position to the Rishi Pahar Mountain is nearly half a kilometer and the length of the mountain is almost the same, it is five hundred steps.' With a sharp-edged stone, he cleared a patch on the ground to fashion his design. His hand engraved these details into the ground as he spoke.

The young soldier knelt beside the ancient Arjuna tree, nearly aligned with the distant Shiva temple, and firmly planted a stick in the ground, marking the spot where their first treasure chest would rest, to be buried at least four feet beneath the earth's surface and marked point A.

'Where is the first treasure?' Asked the young soldier to take confirmation of his communication clarity.

'It is in a straight line from the temple on Rishi Pahar Mountain, at a point half a kilometer faraway and specifically under the Arjuna tree.' Replied one soldier.

From the point A, the young soldier detailed the plan to conceal the treasure within the forest. He carefully selected twenty locations, which, when deciphered, would serve as a hidden code to reveal their whereabouts. This intricate system ensured that only those with the knowledge and insight to decode the clues could unearth the concealed riches.

Rishabha, their leader, pondered the next crucial element. 'But what about the code? How do we reveal it to our people, young soldier?'

The young soldier shared his ingenious solution, 'Each of us will carry one treasure jar and bury it four feet deep at the spot assigned to each one ensuring the iron ring is set just a few inches below the ground. Once the task is complete, you run to the nearest hamlet or village or you home and share the code that I'm about to disclose.'

He continued, ' Look, the codes can be of many types, it might be a map, it might be the shadows and time based, it might be the knowledge sharing among some limited people which is passed on very carefully from one person to another and some are puzzle based. Our code here is a puzzle in the form of a story.'

The soldiers, now fully engaged, leaned in, eager to hear the code. It came in the form of a concise narrative:

The young soldier detailed the code in the form of a story, 'Enticed by the prince, we embarked on a mission to seize the treasure, promised for the peasants' good. As our journey progressed, a sinister plot was revealed, exposing the prince's intent to poison us and claim the treasure. At last, upon reaching Rishi Pahar Mountain, we beseeched Lord Shiva for his divine aid. Answering our plea, Lord Shiva appeared with a bow as high as the sky and concealed the treasures using a mountain-sized massive serpent as his arrow. The serpent clutched all the treasure jars with its fangs, and upon Lord Shiva's command, it sailed through the forest, secreting away the treasures deep under the soil, with the iron ring a few inches below the ground. *The clue to find the spots is the number 707.*'

Though they couldn't understand the number 707, the soldiers were taken aback by the young soldier's creativity and couldn't help but break into applause. Encouraged by their appreciation, the young soldier further elaborated, 'As we reveal the code, there might be a chance we miss some part of it, but the crux story for the code is that 'Lord Shiva shot the mountain-sized serpent arrow that buried the treasure across the forest, only a few inches below the ground.' That's the key.'

With Rishabha assigning each soldier to their respective spot according to the diagram, he instructed them to commence their mission.

Before the soldiers dispersed to their designated spots for burying the treasure, Rishabha gathered them for a heartfelt farewell speech. With sincerity in his voice, he addressed his comrades:

'Shivanas, my dear brothers, today we embark on a mission of utmost importance, one that could change the fate of our kingdom and its people. When I say it changes the fate of our kingdom, I don't mean that they would find the treasure and monetize it to buy back their lands. What I find worrying is that people in the kingdom are becoming cowards, I had been expecting a revolution against the king during the drought but no one at least voiced their concerns. Hence my thought is that they may or may not find the treasure but let them understand what needs to be done to own something that belongs to them. Let them know what we sacrificed for. Let them realize their mistakes and may they unite to revolt against the king. And here, we stand united in the face of treachery and adversity, driven by a purpose greater than ourselves. The treacherous poison may course through our veins, but our spirits remain unbroken. As we set forth to hide the treasures bestowed upon us by Lord Shiva, let us remember that our sacrifice today will ensure that these riches benefit the very peasants they were meant for. We bear the weight of this responsibility, knowing that our actions will bring hope to those who have suffered. Let us move with determination and courage, knowing that our bond as brothers will carry us through even the darkest of times. And when the time comes to reveal the code, may our voices echo through the villages, carrying the message of our sacrifice throughout the kingdom. But finally, you all have to excuse me, for I am the reason your families will miss you, for their tears, for their struggles henceforth, for your wife, sons and daughters who will wait for your arrival at the doors, for your parents who will need your support, for your friends who will long for your company.'

Rishabha concluded, his voice firm and resolute, 'My dear soldiers, my Shivanas, remember, when you reveal the code indicating where these treasures are hidden, warn them. That the serpent will haunt those who use the treasure for the personal gain. First, it will haunt them in their dreams and then they wake up to see the serpent coming so close that it licks their cheeks with its venomous fangs, coiling around their necks and chests, crushing them until they gasp for breath, and it becomes their relentless torment until their last breath. And while you speak in the villages and to your family, expose the sinister nature of the prince. A lot to do in the last moment. Farewell, my twenty brave comrades, my brothers. Our clan, the Shivanas, will be remembered for ages.'

Rishibha concluded asking the young soldier to recite a similar poem to instill energy in the team, 'Hey Robert Frost, do you have a poem that suits the occasion.'

When Rishabha requested him to recite a poem, the young soldier found himself unable to utter a single word. A profound cry lay beneath the surface of his emotions, and if he had opened his mouth, only shouts would have erupted. The sole method to rein in his inner turmoil was to counterbalance the weight on his mind with a physical burden. Thus, he walked towards the brass jar, hoisted it onto his shoulder, and turned to face the assembled soldiers, summoning all his strength to restrain the tears welling up. Swallowing his sorrow and stifling the cry within, he, with quivering lips, recited a poem by Robert Frost.

"Whose woods these are I think I know.
His house is in the village though;
He will not see me stopping here
To watch his woods fill up with snow.

The woods are lovely, dark and deep,
But I have promises to keep,
And miles to go before I sleep,
And miles to go before I sleep."

Later, each soldier set out on a solo journey to the treasure spots assigned to them.

On the way Rishabha addressed the young soldier, his tone both somber and compassionate. 'I have a suggestion. I would take the burden of your treasure jar and have a task for you my friend. You are the youngest one here and you are the bread-winner of your family. I know you have a younger sister who awaits for you. I suggest you go home and ask them to leave the village and take refuge in any other kingdom for a while. Later you will have some time to be the harbinger of our code to as many people as possible. Spread the word far and wide, but also be vigilant. Warn them of the serpent's curse, and ensure that this treasure serves the greater good.'

The young soldier nodded, understanding the weight of the responsibility entrusted to him. Before the young soldier left, Rishabha broke one of the treasure jars and handed over some gold coins, to the young soldier and asked him to give it to his sister. With that, the young soldier set off on his mission, while Rishabha began his laborious journey to hide the treasure in its secret locations, deep within the dense forest.

All the soldiers after burring the treasure jars, they continued to the nearby villages, some visited their families and with serious belief, they shared the mysterious code, told the scary tale of the serpent's curse and exposed the nature of the prince.

As they completed their duty with firm determination, destiny had a continuation plan for them. One after another, like falling blocks, the soldiers surrendered to the harmful poison flowing in their veins. The deadly substance began to show its evil effects. Their skin, once healthy and full of life, turned pale and grayish, taking on a peculiar bluish tint. Their breaths became shallow and difficult, as if the very air they breathed was against them. In the midst of suffering, they held onto their chests, struggling to take the precious breaths that were slipping away.

Their courageous hearts, which had beaten strongly with unwavering determination, now weakened, and the world around them slowly faded into darkness. The once-mighty soldiers, who had set out on a mission to protect their kingdom's treasures, now lay motionless.

The events that unfolded didn't stay hidden for long. Word quickly reached the ears of the king, and the prince's devious plot was exposed for all to see. The prince, gripped by fear and shame, found himself in a situation where he could no longer face his father or the kingdom. His only option was to flee into exile, leaving behind his life of luxury and privilege.

King Yasho Mardhana, a ruler who had always been solely concerned with his own reputation, wealth, and personal gain, was now faced with the stark reality that his actions had brought shame to his family and cast a dark cloud over the entire kingdom. The news of his family's disgrace spread like wildfire, and the neighboring kings who had once held the royal family in high regard now disdained him.

Families, friends, and villagers who had directly heard the soldiers' revelations began to mobilize. This was an unprecedented revolt against the king, a monarch who had never faced such opposition before. The people were determined to hold him accountable for the heinous crimes committed by his own son.

Desperate to suppress the growing unrest, the king sought the assistance of the British army, hoping to use their might to suppress the rebellion that was swelling within his own kingdom. In an attempt to maintain control, he imposed strict curfews across the land, hoping to prevent large gatherings of protestors. The immediate families of the twenty one soldiers migrated the very next day fearing the punishment and revenge from the king.

But in not more than a week, with the revelation of the heinous plot and the cruel fate that had befallen the brave soldiers, a sense of unease began to pervade even among the king's own military. As the story of the poisoned soldiers spread, it became clear that their own comrades had not only been involved but had suffered the tragic fate. This revelation sent shockwaves through the military ranks, sowing seeds of doubt and mistrust. Some soldiers openly expressed their discontent, refusing to carry out orders from a king who had shown such disregard for the lives of his own men. Others quietly began to withdraw their support, unwilling to be associated with a regime stained by deception. The king, already facing a revolt from his subjects, now had to contend with a fractured military, further weakening his grip on power.

Despite the oppressive curfew imposed by the narcissistic king, the military of the kingdom found themselves unable to ignore the tragic fate of the twenty one soldiers who had been poisoned under the prince's sinister plan. Soldiers, who had once stood loyally by the king's side, now felt a profound moral obligation to honor their fallen comrades. They could not let their fellow soldiers be denied a proper funeral and the respect they deserved.

One day, under the hues of a late evening which was competing with the arrival of night, groups of military personnel began to gather at the Rishi Pahar Mountain. Word of this covert assembly spread like ripples in a pond, and soon, a sizable congregation of soldiers had gathered. They whispered to each other in hushed tones, sharing stories of the fallen soldiers and the injustice that had befallen them. The soldiers, standing in a tight formation, facing the temple wall, saluted their fallen brethren – assuming one of the walls symbolize the brave souls.

The military's defiant act sent a powerful message not only to the king but to the entire kingdom. It was a collective declaration that honor, justice, and the memory of their fallen comrades mattered more than blind loyalty to a ruler who had lost his way.

The king, witnessing the soldiers' unwavering commitment to justice, realized that he could not suppress the collective will of his military. The soldiers, with heads held high, carried out the last rites with utmost dignity.

This concealed funeral not only provided closure for the grieving military but also served as a symbol of resistance against a tyrannical ruler. The echoes of that night resonated throughout the kingdom, sowing the seeds of change and inspiring others to challenge the oppressive regime that had held them captive for far too long.

They expressed their collective resolve to provide their comrades with a dignified farewell but as the news of the funeral spread, the Rishi Pahar mountain was filled with people who came to salute the soldiers, almost every man in the kingdom visited the mountain and in salutation, every man brought a bowl of red paint and spilled it on the mountain. By the morning, the entire mountain became red in parallel to the sun. From the mountain, the peasants in the entire kingdom, who lost the land to moneylenders gathered in the village of Jhagaaram. The peasants, now a formidable force, stormed the homes of the moneylenders. They ransacked these houses, and destroyed the documents, contracts, and other records that were incriminating. The peasants not only sought to reclaim what was rightfully theirs but also took control of the land ownership documents. This act was strategic, as it left the moneylenders without leverage or collateral. Faced with the fury of the peasants, the moneylenders realized that they were vulnerable and to flight away from the kingdom was the only option left for them.

Later, in the kingdom, fueled by grief, the aggrieved populace embarked on an extensive search for the treasure throughout the mountainous terrain. Their quest led them to scour every inch of the landscape surrounding the mountain, driven by a determination to expose the elusive secret. After exhaustive efforts, they stumbled upon a concealed brass jar buried a few hundred meters from the mountain at a spot aligned straight to the temple located on the Rishi Pahar Mountain. This jar, hidden just beneath the ground, had an iron ring barely inches below the surface. It served as the first marker laid by the soldiers, indicating the starting point of the route to other treasure spots. In salutation to the soldiers, the populace erected a towering pillar at the very spot where they discovered this significant piece of their history.

The sacrifice of the twenty-one soldiers had served the purpose in just a day.

In the wake of the tragic sacrifice of the twenty-one soldiers, the memory of their valor and the injustice they endured became a heartbreaking and enduring legacy. Each year, as the seasons cycled through, the nearby villages, particularly the village of Jhagaaram to which the Rishi Pahar Mountain belongs to, united in a spirited commemoration of the soldiers' unwavering dedication to justice.

The heart of this annual celebration was none other than the revered Rishi Pahar Mountain and the towering pillar, which had become a symbol of resilience, defiance, and the triumph of good over evil. The mountain, once the setting of a treacherous plan, now stood as a tribute to the soldiers' sacrifice and the enduring power of unity.

One of the central rituals of this celebration was spilling the red paint on the mountain, on the towering pillar and the burning of an effigy representing the nefarious prince who had orchestrated the soldiers' poisoning. The effigy, meticulously crafted by skilled artisans, bore a striking likeness to the prince, complete with his regal attire and a malevolent expression. It was a symbolic act of justice, a way for the villagers to channel their collective anger and frustration at the unjust acts committed against their heroes.

Every year the day of the festival dawned with an air of anticipation and excitement. The villagers, dressed in their traditional attire, gathered at the base of Rishi Pahar. Colorful banners and flags fluttered in the breeze, and the sound of traditional music and folk songs filled the air. A sense of unity pervaded the crowd, as they remembered the soldiers.

Year after year, the festival at Rishi Pahar continued, serving as a powerful reminder that the bonds of community, the pursuit of justice, and the memory of those who had sacrificed their lives would forever be celebrated and cherished. The legacy of the twenty-one soldiers had become a beacon of hope, inspiring generations to come to uphold the values of honor, unity, and resilience.

On the other side, the king, Raja Yasho Mardhana was experiencing something that he never did. No one in the kingdom cooperated to be a part of the administration, the king had the support of the British military only to take up the small administrative tasks. Finally, when the British left India in 1947, King Yasho Mardhana too left with them along with Nishitha Varshini. The British military and officers who were his friends helped him transfer the remaining treasures to England and supported him to reside and sustain the luxury. Before Yasho Mardhana left, he gifted some of his loyal families with significant amounts of gold and asked them to support him in whatever the ways they can to save his name and fame in the kingdom even in his absence. His only plea was to stop the real story and re write the narrative in his favour so that the next generations at least remember him as a good king.

That faction of staunch royal supporters embarked on a mission to rewrite the narrative, crafting a twisted version of events that aimed to glorify the king and vilify the twenty one soldiers who had made the ultimate sacrifice.

These supporters, driven by their unwavering loyalty to the monarchy, propagated a web of fabricated stories and half-truths. They hailed the king as a strategist who had masterminded the entire mission to reclaim the kingdom's treasure from alleged traitors. In their distorted accounts, the soldiers were portrayed as disloyal conspirators who had plotted against the throne.

False tales of the king's supposed heroism began to circulate widely. They claimed that the king had singlehandedly outsmarted a formidable band of rebels, spoiling their nefarious plans and ensuring the safe return of the kingdom's wealth. The supporters lauded him for his 'swift and just' action in dealing with those who had dared to challenge his authority.

In these alternative narratives, the soldiers were depicted as turncoats who had betrayed their king and country for personal gain. Their sacrifices were conveniently ignored, and their memory was tarnished with accusations of betrayal. The royalists hailed the king's actions as a resounding victory for the monarchy, celebrating his smart and decisiveness.

These revisionist accounts of history were disseminated through various means—oral traditions, pamphlets, and even dramatic performances that portrayed the king as a triumphant hero. They aimed not only to rewrite the events but also to rewrite the collective memory of the kingdom, erasing the sacrifices of the twenty one soldiers and glorifying the monarchy.

The celebrations orchestrated by the fervent supporters of the royal family were held within the grand walls of the royal fort. As the years passed and their revisionist version of history gained momentum, the fort became a symbolic center for their gatherings, festivities, and tributes to the king.

Every year, on the anniversary of the events that had emerged at Rishi Pahar Mountain, the royal supporters converged on the fort to commemorate what they saw as a momentous victory for the monarchy. The fort's imposing gates would swing open to welcome a procession of loyalists, draped in the royal colors and bearing banners and portraits of the king.

The festivities within the fort were a spectacle. Elaborate decorations adorned its ancient walls, depicting scenes of valor and the king's supposed triumph over the so-called traitors. Musicians played triumphant melodies, and dancers performed choreographed routines that celebrated the monarchy's greatness. In the heart of the fort's courtyard, a grand stage was erected, featuring dramatic reforms of the events, with a highly embellished narrative that favored the king. Skilled actors played the roles of the soldiers, portraying them as deceitful rebels, while the king's character was cast as a wise and heroic ruler.

The GOST troop wrapped up the performance, and as the enthralling play concluded, the crowd began to disperse, engaging in lively conversations with one another. It was a norm that at the end of the show while all start to disperse, Ravidasa switches off all the lights on the stage and only let his voice to be heard to beg every one with a message.

'Oh, they too had families waiting for them, families who longed for their return. They knew, yet, with hearts burdened by the weight of love, they made the ultimate sacrifice. The thoughts of sons and daughters, mothers and fathers flickered through their minds. They knew what they were about to lose.

Oh, how they wept! Their cries echoed through the vast expanse of the forest, reverberating in every corner. The birds in the sky, the creatures of the wild—each one bore witness to their painful screams. But we, we have turned a deaf ear. We have chosen to be insensible to the tales of anguish told by mothers and fathers who witnessed their sons gulping for breathe. Our ears refuse to carry the desperate pleas of wives who suffered in unending sorrow until their last breath. We deny entrance to our minds, the haunting images of those innocent children—the ones who couldn't shed tears and continuously sought answers from their mothers, yearning to know the whereabouts of their absent fathers. In our apathy, we have turned a blind eye, discarding the sacrifices, the grief, and the shattered lives left behind. It is time to lend our ears, open our hearts, and honor the fallen heroes whose cries remain unheard in our deafened world.

Yeah, the men and women of Vijetha mandala, don't you have the responsibility to stand for their sacrifice, don't you feel for those who tried and died for your ancestors, don't you shed tears for their sacrifice. Let's question ourselves, why only a few should venture into the death zones while others wine and dine with friends and families.

Dear all the villagers of Jhagaram, the real men and women, go in search of the treasure chests and find one to prove the story and force the state to honor them officially. Let the sacrifice be written on stones and passed on to generations, for it is the least that we can do to honor the sacrifice.'

Aditya walked back home with a heart burdened by a blend of emotions. Attended many times with interest but this time he had paid keen attention to that theatrical performance that stirred in him the emotions which he had when he was in teens – a compassion towards the twenty one soldiers. As he made his way through the bustling streets, he couldn't help but overhear fragments of conversations about treasure stories.

Among the crowd, a young teenager turned to his older brother and inquired, 'Brother, what should one do if he found a treasure chest?' The brother chuckled and replied, 'Give it to me, and I'll give you anything you want.' A random neighbor in the crowd couldn't resist interjecting, 'Don't share the news with anyone, not even your brother. Ha-ha!'

With curiosity, another voice from the crowd asked, 'Well, what do you expect the person to do then?' From somewhere within the crowd, a response emerged, 'Just keep it to yourself.' Laughter erupted as another voice chimed in, 'And beware, the snakes will come for the treasure and take you too, hahaha!'

Aditya listened intently to these conversations, finding solace in overhearing as he had no one to converse with along the way. His friends seemed to have disappeared into the sea of people, and he had little interest in searching for them amidst the bustling crowd.

Within the chatter, an unaware guest approached the immediate person walking with Aditya, 'I'm curious and seriously asking, what does one do if they stumble upon a treasure?' got a reply, 'There is a person named Prakash Devan, who leads the Shivan's movement. Anyone who accidentally discovers the treasure should inform him personally. However no one can venture for treasure hunting into the forest as it is illegal.'

Intrigued, the guest asked, 'Where does Prakash Devan reside?' The family responded, 'He lives in the capital city and is a well-known businessman cum activist.' Curiosity getting the better of him, the guest inquired further, 'What does he do once he is informed?' The other side explained, 'His plan is to open the treasure in the presence of the general public, the media, the district collector, and elected representatives. This way, no one can deviate, disagree, or exert influence on the discovery. If did so, then the government would declare the valor of soldiers is true and officially search for the remaining treasure jars. This is the objective of the Shivan's Pride movement.'

'How about the families of the twenty one soldiers? They might know exact details.' He extended his thoughts.

'From the very year, 1945, when the treasure was buried by the soldiers, there were adventurers and the enthusiasts who tried to decode the puzzled story of treasure. In the process, what every new adventurer and a new enthusiast did was to meet the family members of those twenty one soldiers. The families and the extended families of those soldiers were traced to get the first hand information and to listen to the code and inquire if any more clues persisted with them. Except the youngest soldier's, the families of the twenty brave soldiers were traced and those families became well known across the erstwhile region of Vijetha Mandala. Those families too grew tired of the constant visits from curious folks who wanted to hear the code repeated over and over again. To put an end to the never-ending requests, they decided to write down what they had heard directly from the soldiers and wrote it on their walls. ***Upon reaching Rishi Pahar Mountain, we beseeched Lord Shiva for his divine aid.***

Answering our plea, Lord Shiva appeared with a bow as high as the sky and concealed the treasures using the mountain-sized massive serpent as his arrow. The serpent clutched all the treasure jars with its fangs, and upon Lord Shiva's command, it sailed through the forest, secreting away the treasures deep under the soil, with the iron ring few inches below the ground. The clue to find the spots is the number 707. However, there was still one mystery left: the family of the youngest soldier. From the little hints and pieces of information the other twenty soldiers had given before they died, it seemed that the youngest among them was the one who had guided the team in hiding of the treasure and had also created the complicated code protecting it. Many tried to find the family of this young soldier, but they couldn't. It appeared that the family had disappeared on the same day the soldiers came back home. There was one person who had seen closely what happened that day, a neighbor of the young soldier's family. Through that person what everyone knew was that the young soldier who returned home from the forest after being poisoned, revealed the code, wrote it on his sister's slate, made everyone who gathered around to mug it up the code like a hymn. Later, he gave a leather bag to his family and asked them to leave the kingdom fearing the king but before they left, the soldier whispered something to his family. After the family left the kingdom, the loyalists to the king attempted to trace them, but a year later, a rumor circulated that the family had met an untimely demise.' Detailed an elderly enthusiast in the crowd.

As Aditya continued his journey, the random conversations echoed through the dimly lit streets, illuminated by the gentle glow of the half-moon. What Aditya heard on the walk back was nothing new. The crowd gradually dispersed as the side streets indicated. But anything related to the story of Shivanas or treasure would create a whirlpool of emotions in Aditya as his father flashes on his mind.

As Aditya aged after his father Raghava's demise in 1985, the burning desire to avenge his father's killers persisted. The memories of those final weeks before his father's demise remained etched in Aditya's mind, replaying like a haunting reel in his thoughts each day. He could still feel the exhilaration of being swung high in the air, the warmth of his father's embrace as he cuddled him to sleep, the routine morning ritual of being dropped off at school with a gentle smile, and the simple joys of being treated to chocolates—a gesture that, for Aditya, carried profound significance. These memories, though seemingly ordinary, were the threads that wove the fabric of a loving father-son relationship, now preserved in the sanctuary of Aditya's heart.

Even years after the disappearance of Raghava, people would often empathize with Aditya and offer their condolences for the loss that seemed impossible to comprehend. Aditya's thoughts remained fixated on the unresolved questions surrounding his father's fate.

Aditya possessed a handful of provocative clues on who killed his father but lacked the concrete evidence that could unravel the mystery. Whenever the waves of emotions related to his father surged within him, Aditya would seek clarity in the pages of Raghava's diary, reliving and revealing his father's days in the year before he went missing.

As his life consolidated year after year, after his father's demise, the only purpose he felt of his life was to unravel the mystery surrounding his father's demise, punish the culprits and take up the mission of Shivan's Pride that fought to restore the sacrifice of the twenty one soldiers. Hence whenever there was any gathering or discussion or stage shows related to Shivanas, Aditya would never miss.

The igniting story of bee keeper

In the year 1980

Following the royals' exit from the land after Independence, two distinct factions – royal supporters and soldiers' sympathizers - continued to commemorate their versions and to celebrate with the themes that supported their thoughts.

Yet, irrespective of which side they championed, a shared fascination had gripped the entire population. The talk of the town was all about a hidden treasure deep within the forest. This treasure had captured the curiosity and dreams of everyone in the land.

The search for this hidden fortune had become something of a cultural norm. People formed groups, united by their shared pursuit, while a few others chose a solitary path, venturing deep into the dense woods. Some wealthy royal loyalists even provided financial support to these treasure-hunting expeditions, fueling the fervor.

Each treasure seeker had their interpretation of the story, and the code, and the quest had become an emergency, with enthusiasts from all walks of life attempting to piece it together. Experts were consulted to decode the cryptic hints that lay within the tale, and priests were called upon to invoke divine guidance in the pursuit. Yet, despite their efforts, the treasure remained a puzzle.

A few deciphered the code to conclude that the treasure was somewhere in the mountain that spread five hundred meters. Those who believed this searched every possible space and gaps between the rocks, ventured deep into the caves, dug wherever there was soil but none could succeed.

As there was snake and arrow, a few decoded the puzzle that the treasure was hidden under the Arjuna tree where there were snake burrows. Those believed this dug every snake burrow they came across.

A few believed that the treasure was thrown in the lake which was one kilometer away from the Rishi Pahar mountain – as lord Shiva has also a symbol of Ganga. The clue 707 was perceived as the distance in various measurements from centimeters to meters along the Rishi Pahar Mountain.

As time passed, and yet the treasure stayed hidden, the initial excitement and enthusiasm about the quest started to fade. With each journey into the forest that didn't reveal the hidden wealth, the hope of finding it grew dimmer. As the seasons changed and time moved on, the desire to search for the treasure became less. The stories of unsuccessful attempts and the forest's mysteries turned the once-exciting quest into a distant memory. Slowly, fewer and fewer people were willing to go into the forest to look for the mysterious treasure.

However, there was one individual who had been persistently searching for the treasure, all while maintaining his beekeeping profession, for nearly a decade.

Naagam, one of the finest beekeepers in the erstwhile Vijetha mandala, was also a passionate treasure hunter. This unique combination allowed him to navigate the realms of bee hunting and treasure hunting simultaneously. Armed with a long iron stick sharpened at one end and tines to act as a rake at another end, Naagam ventured into the dense forests, with his aluminum can poised to collect the sweet spoils of his beekeeping endeavors and also a sickle for multipurpose use.

In his pockets, he carried a collection of matchsticks and beedis – the handmade cigars - for a smoke during his expeditions. With the beekeeping suit made of jute, neatly folded and secured in a bag, Naagam embarked on his quest to collect honey and in the process to search for the iron ring.

Naagam, the seasoned beekeeping professional, was highly sought after for guidance, not only in locating beehives but also in marketing honey product in the nearby town. Drawing from years of beekeeping experience, Naagam employed various techniques to track the flight patterns and buzzing sounds of the bees. He possessed a keen eye for detail, through countless endeavors, Naagam honed his tracing skills, becoming a master at unraveling the mysteries hidden within the forest.

When Naagam chanced upon a beehive, he would diligently prepare the ground beneath the tree. With his iron rake, he cleared away any debris, ensuring a clean surface for his work. A jute cloth layered with a soft cotton cloth above was carefully spread, guarding against any contamination of honey with mud or leaves. And as he tended to his preparations, his keen gaze remained fixed on the ground, hoping to catch a glimmer of the sought-after iron ring.

Clad in protective clothing that shielded his entire body, Naagam would set his plan into motion. Gathering a bundle of thin branches, he ignited a fire, releasing smoke that would gently dispersed the bees away, allowing him to harvest the honey with ease. While some trees warranted his climbing skills, he preferred to avoid it whenever possible, mindful of the leg cramps that plagued him during such endeavors.

With each honeycomb carefully severed and squeezed into his aluminum can, Naagam collected his golden treasure and made his way back home. But before his return, he made sure he raked the ground few inches to test for the presence of any iron ring. It has become a routine for Naagam to first collect the honey and then scribble with an iron rake a few inches deep the ground to test his luck in striking his rake with the iron ring.

The allure of selling the honey never troubled him, for its demand was limitless. Twice a month, he embarked on a journey to the cities, where eager customers eagerly awaited his arrival, ready to purchase his delicious honey in generous quantities.

Whenever Naagam returned home from his forest expeditions, his family and friends would playfully tease him, wondering if he had stumbled upon any hidden treasure during his adventures. They would jokingly ask if the contents of his aluminum can were honey or gold, as his reputation as a treasure hunter had become synonymous with his name. Much like Lord Shiva wielded a trishul, Naagam always carried his trusty iron rake whenever he ventured into the forest. The iron rake became his symbol of determination and exploration, a tool that accompanied him on his quest through the dense wilderness.

Nearly a decade of his experience, Naagam succeeded in discovering hundreds of beehive spots to cultivate but failed to notice the one iron ring. Years passed and people lost all hopes, both the factions withdrew all the troops almost, the individual enthusiasts stopped long back to think of the treasure hunting and started to focus on real business.

It was then, that Naagam's unfortunate moment happened in the year 1980, during the spring time. Beneath the sheltering branches of a massive Arjuna tree, Naagam carefully knelt down, his hands expertly working to extract every precious drop of honey from the honeycomb he retrieved from the challenging branch of the tree. For Naagam, the act of collecting honey had transformed from a thrilling accomplishment to just another part of his daily life, like any other ordinary routine. The extraordinary had become ordinary, and the excitement that once danced in his eyes was now replaced by the steady rhythm of routine. With the honey safely collected, Naagam's gaze shifted to his trusty iron rake, the tool that had accompanied him through countless journeys. As was his habit, he began tilling and scratching the soil around the Arjuna tree, a routine that had become as innate to him as hunting the honey.

On that day, not so long after he started using the rake against the soil that he found an iron ring struck between the tines of the iron rake. And yes, Naagam's heart skipped a beat, his hands tightening around the handle of the rake as he leaned into the soil. A rush of emotions swept over him, carefully he reached out to the iron rake to hold the object of his relentless quest, the iron ring. To confirm him, the iron ring also revealed its chain that takes him to the treasure chest which is his ultimate quest.

That day, amidst the calm woods, three kilometers far from the village, Naagam felt certain no one was near to his sight or sound nor the path he travelled was a regular one. The sun hung high in the sky, reminded him the ample time he had before dusk and his family, long back stopped predicting his time of return from his work.

Putting back the iron ring with chain back on the ground, Naagam surveyed around for some bushes and hid all his belongings in it and made some space for him behind the bushes to refugee himself in case of any unexpected visitor. Naagam then approached the iron ring kneeling down, he held it, the nearly half a feet diameter ring with one inch thickness, attached to the iron chain. Naagam passed his hands from the ring to the chain, held it tightly and pulled it with all his strength but the chain resisted. Naagam stood gripping the iron ring and used all his strength but only blisters were seen on his hands, not even an inch of the chain moved forward. He then took the rake and used the other side which acted as a dagger and started to dig the area along the chain. But the summer hardened the soil making it tough to the dagger to break the compacted soil to chunks. After every few minutes, he swept away the chunks to clear the way along the chain so that he can dig deeper till the treasure chest. The toughened ground made his work so tedious that it took one hour to dig a feet into the ground along the chain. Naagam felt exhausted, sat under the tree for a while and went into the bush to get his belongings. He spread the jute mat on the exposed ring and chain, and sat on it to have his food and water. He started analyzing that if with the same pace he carried out the excavation, it would take hours to dig three more feet and the quality of tools is in no competition with the compactness of the soil. Naagam felt the need to moisture the soil and tougher tools to dig. After having all the arguments in himself, Naagam decided to visit the site the next day with suitable tools.

It was a prolonged dusk due to the summer arrival and Naagam made his appearance in the village when the fading light of the dusk was dancing across the streets he walked. He walked faster while anxiety filled his face and pace. Bearing the heavy honey can on the head with a hand and another hand holding the beekeeping suit, rake and other tools, Naagam rushed towards his house. He tried to be normal with every greeting and joke he had along the way. People noticed the anxiety on his face and walk but attributed it to the heaviness of the honey can.

But Naagam was carrying more weight inside his head than that of on his head. The physical weight of the honey can, the pain on the hands due to blisters went unfelt by him. He became insensitive to the physical world and by the time he reached his house he hardly remembered whom he greeted or was greeted by along the way. Standing at the main door bearing the weights on the head and in the hands, he shouted for his wife who rushed and with a practiced ease took the honey can from his head to place it in the corner meant for it. His three sons below twelve years, playing in the backyard were quick to sense his return, dashed towards him to enquire the honey.

Naagam set the portable fabric netted cot and sat on it in silence. While his wife was preparing the kerosene lamp to make it ready when the darkness falls. The lamp was crafted from an upcycled medicine glass bottle. It featured a metal cap with a passageway for a twisted cotton thread that extended into the bottle. When filled with kerosene, this simple setup transformed the bottle into a functional lamp. For every three to four days, the kerosene was added to the bottle and his wife was doing the same.

'Father, how much honey did you collect today?' The innocent question came from one of his three sons, all below twelve years of age.

'Enough for now. Run along and play,' Naagam replied, his fatigue evident.

'Can we see it, Dad?' another son chimed in eagerly and ran near the can to open it.

'Hands off! Go to the backyard and play there,' he responded sternly, asserting his authority.

His wife joined the conversation, her voice gentle and rational. 'Boys, leave your father alone for a bit. He might need to rest. You can check the honey later.'

Placing the lamp in the lamp shelf, Naagam's wife went to the back side of the house to the place meant to cook using earthen stove. Tucked in a corner between the house and the compound wall, the setup for earthen stove stood at a modest one feet in height and four feet in width. Its construction resembled a cubicle, with the house and the compound wall serving as two of its enclosing sides.

She made a bed of small sticks in the stove and lit it, while the flames spread, she went to bring water in the metal boiler. As she was placing maize stocks to increase the flame, Naagam neared her and helped her put the boiler on the stove.

Immediately after adjusting the boiler properly on the uneven earthen stove, Naagam sat at the stove and held her hand and pulled her to sit there itself, signaling there was something urgent to be discussed. She never experienced such actions from him and she sat with a mix of emotions.

'Dear, I have something important to share, but let's keep it between us for now. Today, while I was out collecting honey, I stumbled upon a significant discovery – a massive iron ring attached to a long, sturdy chain beneath the tree,' Naagam whispered to his wife, his voice tinged with a mixture of excitement and nervousness.

'Wait, what did you say? Can you repeat that?' his wife urged, her eyes widening in surprise.

'I said I found a big iron ring connected to a chain,' Naagam repeated, making sure his words were clear.

'Did you see the treasure chest too?' she inquired, her voice hushed.

'I tried to dig, but the ground was so hard. I couldn't budge the chain even an inch,' Naagam admitted, his face reflecting a blend of determination and frustration.

'How deep were you able to dig?' she questioned, a note of concern in her voice.

'I managed to get down about two feet before it became nearly impossible,' Naagam replied, meeting his wife's gaze squarely.

'From what we've heard, the chest is said to be buried around four feet down,' she pointed out.

'That's right,' Naagam confirmed.

'Have you told anyone else about this?' she probed, worry evident in her tone.

'No, I made sure not to share a word with anyone on my way back,' Naagam reassured her.

'Okay, so what's your plan now?' she asked, leaning in slightly, intrigued.

Naagam leaned closer, his words barely more than a whisper. 'Here's what I'm thinking – every day, I'll bring home a small amount of gold, concealed within the honey. I'll also stash some gold within the folds of my beekeeping suit. Once I'm home and the kids are asleep, we can carefully transfer the gold from the honey and hide it in the grain bin. What do you think?'

His wife nodded thoughtfully. 'That sounds like a solid plan, but I believe it might be best to send the children to my mother's village for a while.'

Naagam's brow wrinkled. 'How can we manage that? We can't leave right now, and the trip takes three days at least.'

'No need to worry, I can arrange for a cart and send your cousin along to accompany them. I'll just tell everyone I'm not feeling well to take care of them,' she suggested.

'Sounds like a clever plan,' Naagam agreed.

'However, I do have another concern,' his wife confessed, a touch of worry coloring her voice.

'What's bothering you?' Naagam inquired, intrigued by her tone.

'Well, you know the legend about snakes guarding hidden treasures? I think we should be extra careful starting tomorrow,' she cautioned, her eyes locked onto his, filled with caution and care.

'Let us not discuss anything in front of kids today and try not to meet neighbors frequently for some days, unintentionally we show our anxiety.' Naagam suggested.

'I am sure about this.' She replied and it's been long that the water got hot enough.

Armed with a sense of purpose, Naagam prepared for his next venture into the forest. This time, he went more prepared - a hammer, a small digging bar and a shovel, a pot along with his regular tools - the beekeeping suit, mat and the can for honey. He had to start very early to execute his plan. One was to ensure no one noticed him carrying so many tools and another is that he needs to walk additional distance to pool water in the can and the pot to wet the spot.

As he ventured to the spot beneath the neem tree, the same place where fate had revealed the iron ring to him, his heart raced with a mix of anticipation and caution.

Naagam placed all the tools in the bush and carried the empty pot and the can to the pond which was nearly two kilometers away from the spot but it was worth it to make his job easier.

Bearing the pot on his shoulder supported by a hand and the honey can on another hand he returned to the spot. Resting for few minutes, Naagam commenced his work. Placing the digging bar tip firmly into the soil, he raised the hammer high above and struck the dagger with controlled force. As the sound echoed in the forest, Naagam tied a piece of cloth on the top of the digging bar and continued. Inch by inch, the bar pierced the ground, creating a series of holes and once a few hole were created, he poured water into them slowly and carefully to reduce the wastage.

The cycle continued - bar strikes, followed by the careful infusion of water. His hands grew hard, his body weary, but his resolve never wavered. Once he felt enough of the soil got moist, he dug the place using the bar and the shovel, his work got easy that way. But he could do it easily only till the depth where water got infused. And again he started the cycle - bar strikes, careful infusion of water.

After three cycles, while he was digging, the bar made an unusual sound and the metal bar had stopped to penetrate. Naagam used a shovel to clear the mud chunks and the moment had come to witness the wonder, a fragment of something different, something that broke the monotony of the black soil. Carefully, he cleared the dirt away, revealing a hint of a rusty-colored surface. He finally won the hide and seek game after ten years.

With a renewed sense of urgency, Naagam's hands worked with a wild excitement. He dug around the exposed part of the jar and kept on clearing and then, there it was - the opening of the jar, tightly sealed with a cap and screws.

His breath caught as he examined the jar more closely. The cap was fixed securely to the body with screws. Determined Naagam reached for the hammer and with a calculated precision, he worked to loosen the screws that held the cap in place.

The cap had four screws and Naagam smashed one after the other. As the final screw gave way, Naagam's heart raced. He carefully removed the cap, his hands trembling with a mixture of apprehension and awe. And then, his eyes fell upon it - a sight that left him momentarily breathless. Gold, gleaming and precious, lay nestled within the jar, a treasure trove of unbearable weight physically and mentally. His hands trembled as he reached into the jar, carefully lifting a piece of gold, letting its weight and significance sink in. And as he stood there, in the heart of the forest, holding a piece of gold in his hands, Naagam couldn't help but feel that the journey had been worth every moment of his determination and patience.

Naagam carefully scooped the gold biscuits out of the jar, transferring them into the honey can that he had brought along. At that moment, the can was partially filled with water. He felt he was expressing his gratitude to Goddess Lakshmi, by washing the biscuits in water. Then, he began distributing them into different hiding spots. Some found their way into the floor mat, while a few were carefully tucked into the pockets of his beekeeping suit. The rest remained nestled in the can. He packed the floor mat and the beekeeping suit in a separate cloth bag that had handles made of thin ropes.

Naagam was thorough. He didn't want any jingling sound by the gold in the can while he walked. So, he filled the can further, but this time with honey he had brought along in smaller containers. This masked any noise the gold might make while moving. With everything set and his secret securely stashed away, he felt a sense of cautious triumph.

Having meticulously transferred what might have been around ten percent of the treasure into the honey can and into other places, Naagam resealed the jar. The iron ring and chain found their place again, concealing the secret with a blanket of loose soil. This preparation was concluded well before noon, leaving him with ample time until his planned departure in the evening. He had purposefully chosen that timing to avoid encounters with fellow villagers who might want to chat or inquire about his honey, as often happened in their tight-knit community.

With his preparations complete, he resolved to have lunch and perhaps catch a brief nap before his departure. However, before he could carry out this plan, he checked on his hidden belongings, ensuring that they were safely concealed beneath the bush, hidden from any wandering eyes.

Opening his lunchbox, Naagam found his simple yet comforting meal of curd rice and mango pickle. He started to eat but his mind was too preoccupied to eat heartily. He managed to force down a small portion, leaving most of it untouched. His anxiety killed his appetite. The previous night too had been restless, his thoughts oscillating between curiosity about the treasure and the weight of the secret he carried.

After lunch, the same restlessness persisted. His anxiety to finally witness the treasure, combined with the troublesome thoughts of snakes creeping around in the shadows, sent his mind into overdrive. He lay down, attempting to sleep, but each time his eyes closed, his thoughts raced uncontrollably in anxiety. He wetted a towel and draped it over his head, hoping to cool down his feverish mind, but the anticipated relief did not arrive. He made the damp towel into a makeshift pillow, hoping that the change in position would persuade slumber, yet sleep remained distant.

His consciousness swayed between the glittering charm of the treasure and the fear of snakes. Each rustling leaf, every distant sound, sent jolts of alertness through him, making him assume a snake nearby. He found himself constantly scanning above and around him, distinguishing every noise, assessing if it was the hiss of a snake or the scampering of a harmless creature. The forest, teeming with life, played tricks on his senses.

With every passing moment, his vigilance heightened, and his towel became a constant companion as he attempted to find some solace in its cool touch. The minutes slipped by in this state of heightened awareness, and the time for his departure grew nearer. He placed the digging bar and the shovel under the bush as he needed them every day for at least a week more and gathered his belongings to embark on the journey back to the village, his senses still attuned to the slightest disturbance in his surroundings. He pulled the rope handles of the cloth bag together and tied them lest it loose on the way and he held it in one hand while the other hand held the honey can.

With the utmost caution, Naagam retraced his steps through the forest and re-entered the village. This marked the second day he had managed to avoid encountering any villagers along the way. Despite his attempts to appear casual, he couldn't shake off an underlying unease. He walked determinedly, showing artificial smiles for those who greeted him. The customary 'No stock now' was his response to inquiries about honey along the way.

As he reached his home, his wife stood by the door, eagerly waiting for him. Without delay, she relieved him of the honey can, and the two of them hurried to the prayer room. There, they carefully placed all their precious belongings – the honey can, the jute bag – both containing the treasure gold. Returning to their seats near the earthen stove, they settled in.

That evening, his wife closed the main door, a departure from the village norm. Normally, doors remained open when someone was home, a gesture of welcome to any acquaintance. The closed door now signaled an air of secrecy. As they sat together, the water simmered on the stove.

'Is there gold?' she inquired, her eyes revealing both anticipation and excitement.

'Yes, a substantial amount, really a lot of' he replied.

'I've hidden it in the can and in the cloth bag. We can examine it once everyone is asleep.'

'Wow, that's incredible,' she exclaimed, her face lighting up with joy.

'How about the kids, did they go?' he asked, concern etching his brow.

'An hour after you left this morning, your cousin came and took them. I've asked him to stay there with the kids for a week,' she reassured him. Then she asked, 'So, were there any snakes in the treasure chest?'

'No, not at all. I didn't come across any snakes on the way either,' he replied, his voice laced with relief.

'Are you hungry now? Shall I make something?' she inquired gently.

'No, strangely I don't have much of an appetite. I couldn't sleep at all last night, and even during the day, I couldn't eat or rest,' Naagam admitted, his worry evident.

'Stop worrying,' she said, her tone soothing. 'We've been blessed with this treasure. We'll take our time to figure out how to use it wisely.'

His eyes clouded with concern, Naagam added, 'It's not the treasure that's troubling me. I had dreams filled with snakes last night.'

'I'll do something about that,' she replied reassuringly. 'Now, I'll go to the Shiva temple in the village and pray for you. I'll get you a sacred band from the temple. It should bring you some peace.'

Naagam went to take bath and his wife went to the temple to pray and to bring the sacred band and vibhoodhi. But the scariest thing had already happened – the most venomous snake in the forest was inside the rope-handled cloth bag placed in the prayer room, was trying to escape from that bag. The Russel's viper, the most venomous, the dominated snake breed in the forest is considered the deadliest one. Its lethal brown color matched by its zigzag bands on the back and its eyes are voids of wickedness. It swifts that no eye can follow, its attack doesn't give time to get terrified at least. The mere sight of the snake, the stout, muscular and predatory look, is enough to render sleepless nights as it infiltrates even dreams - many claimed sleepless nights after its just sight and said that it appeared close to their faces and they could see the scales of the skin on the triangular head, its unblinking eyes and the warning play of fangs. Its infiltration into dreams was so intense that one would get struck in deciding to open their eyes in fear that they would see the snake eye to eye.

On that important morning, as Naagam dipped the gold biscuits in water and placed them in the pockets of his beekeeping suit and the mat, he unintentionally set a series of events in motion. That action made the wet clothes feel cool, catching the attention of creatures nearby. Without his knowledge, these seemingly harmless actions would lead to an unexpected situation.

The Russel's viper was on the hunt chasing a small mouse, its prey, which rushed desperately toward the bag containing the damp clothes wrapped around the valuable gold. In its pursuit of the mouse, the snake entered the bag, and successfully catching the mouse, the snake was full and typically, after eating, snakes tend to rest for a while. Since the cloth bag felt cool due to its dampness, the snake found it comfortable. Opting for relaxation, it settled deeper into the bag to rest, completely unaware of what was about to happen.

It was only when Naagam picked up the bag in the evening, held the rope handles, and pulled them together to tie them, that the viper felt an uncomfortable pressure. As the handles tightened and the bag closed, the snake suddenly realized that its place of safety had turned into a trap. Surprised, it reacted instinctively, twisting and squirming in the confined space but found it no use.

Naagam had no clue nor had any guess on what happened. While carrying the rope-handled bag, he thought he was holding his fortune rather he was holding his death.

After his strenuous day, Naagam sought solace in a long and soothing bath, the warmth of the water melting away the weariness in his body. He dressed and reclined on the portable netted cot, positioned near the main door, eagerly anticipating his wife's return. Gazing at the clay tiles that formed the roof above him, his thoughts became a whirl of emotions - fear, contentment, anticipation, and his elaborate schemes. He lost so deeply in his thoughts that his senses seemed to desert him - a creature was crawling on his feet but he wasn't aware.

As his wife entered the house, she shouted upon seeing her husband's preoccupied state. It was her shout that jolted Naagam from his trance, and he shivered as he realized a creature had been investigating his feet. Swiftly, his wife armed herself with a broomstick, chasing the intruder away from her husband.

'Lost in thought to the point of not even noticing a mouse biting your feet?' she blamed, taking a seat beside him and whispering her criticism.

'Oh?' Naagam examined his foot, noticing a small scratch. 'No need to worry, it's nothing,' he assured her.

With a sacred band from the temple and a gentle application of vibhoodhi on his forehead, Naagam's wife attended to her husband's well-being. She advised him to rest for a while, leaving him alone.

An hour later, she called him for supper. In response, Naagam promptly rose from the bed and expressed his no appetite state. His wife noticed his promptness and inquired if he hadn't slept.

'As I told you, whenever I close my eyes, I'm confronted by a snake with its head almost touching my forehead and its fangs almost grazing my cheeks,' Naagam explained, his worry evident. 'I don't know how much longer I can bear this burden of treasure.'

'If it distresses you so much, maybe we should consider distributing it to the villagers or even notifying the police,' his wife suggested.

'No, that's not an option. I'm determined to face whatever challenges lie ahead. I've dedicated a decade to this quest, and I can't abandon it now,' Naagam declared resolutely.

Seeking more details, his wife inquired about the precise location of the treasure discovery. Naagam described it meticulously, indicating the entrance to the forest from the west side of the village, the rock formations, the bifurcating road, the route leading to the pond, and the cluster of banyan trees that marked the way.

'Oh, I know that pond. Remember when we went in search of tendu trees?' his wife recollected, referring to her previous venture in search of the leaves used in making hand-rolled cigarettes, known as beedis.

'Yes, exactly. Just two kilometers before that pond, a group of Banyan trees marks the way. At the boundary of this group, concealed behind the Banyan trees, you'll observe a collection of Arjuna trees. One particular tree in their midst appears solitary, encircled by dense bushes,' Naagam reiterated.

Offering to accompany him, disguised as someone seeking tendu trees, his wife suggested a plan for the next day. Naagam considered the proposal, but uncertainty lingered in his response.

'We'll see,' he replied noncommittally, and both of them rose to partake in their supper.

Yet again, Naagam found it difficult to eat much, consumed by the relentless waves of anxiety that had been tormenting his mind.

A few hours later, while everyone in the village was asleep, Naagam and his wife woke up. They went into their prayer room to look at the gold biscuits they had hidden. His wife was really happy. She took the biscuits out of the honey and cleaned them in the backyard and came back to the prayer room. Then, she opened up the cloth bag having the beekeeping suit and the mat to place it on the ground. After that, she put all the gold into a small pot, planning to hide it at the bottom of the grain bin.

Just before they were about to leave the prayer room, something unexpected happened. The snake, which escaped from the cloth bag and now had been trying to crawl through the clay tiles on the roof, slipped and fell on Naagam's head. The snake, frightened and trying to hold on, wrapped itself around Naagam's neck. This scared both Naagam and his wife so much that they screamed. Naagam tried to pull the snake away, but in the process, the snake bit him.

The struggle made Naagam lose his balance, and he fell to the ground. During all this chaos, the pot with the precious gold broke as it hit the floor, and the gold biscuits scattered all over. Naagam's wife rushed out to call their neighbors for help. They all came running, but no one was brave enough to go inside because of the snake.

Unfortunately, Naagam didn't survive that night. The snake's bite was dangerous, but it wasn't the only reason for his death. His heart couldn't handle the anxiety, fear and worry anymore, and it gave out. Hours later after filling the house with fire smoke and ensuring the viper left, the villagers entered the house. Among them, a few carried the body of Naagam and a few lifted the spilled gold.

After Naagam's funeral, his wife found herself in police custody. Pushed by the sway of a local politician, she succumbed to the pressure and disclosed the location of the treasure. Subsequently, the police, along with the politician's associates, raided the spot and seized the loot for themselves. Within days of their covert operation, word spread throughout the village about the treasure's location. However, what gained the most traction was the revelation that the treasure had been distributed between the police and the politician, prompting whispers of doubt and mistrust among the villagers.

Naagam's passing sparked a surge of activity among the people in the nearby regions. Numerous individuals began venturing into the depths of the forest again. Naagam's legacy underscored the strength of unwavering determination; his decade-long pursuit had culminated in the ultimate discovery, a testament to the power of perseverance. However, the cruel twist of fate that led to his demise in the grip of a viper's fangs cast a somber shadow over his triumph.

Inspired by Naagam's story, a wave of young adventurers embarked on their own quests into the forest. Drawn by the tempting prospect of unearthing hidden riches, they sought to follow in his footsteps, each step echoing with the memory of his resolute journey. However, cautioning them to be careful with the vipers, police and the politicians.

Another ugly side of the society was also revealed when everyone, the known and the unknown, the friends and the foes, everyone ransacked the house of Naagam and destroyed the house in the hope to find the treasure in the walls or the roof, under the ground or in the shelves, making the family shelter less. Naagam's family left the village while everyone watched with no guilt.

Revolt and conspiracy – Hand in hand

Between 1980 to 1988

After Naagam's untimely demise proving the presence of treasure, many residents ventured into the dense forests, some in groups, others in isolation, hoping to uncover the hidden riches.

In 1980, among those who embarked on this treasure hunt was Aditya's father, Raghava, a man known for his strong sense of camaraderie and leadership. Raghava joined forces with his close friend, Vikram, appointing him as the leader of their group. Both Vikram and Raghava were in their mid-twenties. While Raghava had a happy home with his wife and mother, Vikram was living with his grandmother as he lost his parents when he was in teens. Since then, Raghava had become the friend, savior and family for Vikram. It was Raghava who helped him in all the ways - morally, financially and friendly. The strength of Raghava had been his mother who built the family from scratch.

As Raghava got married, she accumulated eight acres of land and enough savings for his son to venture into any business. She also took care to bring up her son with values.

In 1980, the very first few days of Raghava's venture into the treasure hunt, his wife gave birth to a healthy baby boy, Aditya, a bundle of joy that brought immense happiness to their household. In those times, the birth of a son was not just a cause for celebration; it was seen as an achievement, a symbol of prosperity, and a source of confidence for a father. The arrival of a son bestowed upon Raghava a renewed sense of purpose and determination added with lot of freedom. With his heart full of paternal pride, he felt bolstered to pursue his dreams, including his newfound interest in the world of business and politics.

In the eyes of the villagers, having a son was considered a stroke of luck, a blessing that negated the need for accumulating wealth. Raghava's political aspirations began to take shape as he actively engaged in community affairs, forging friendships, expanding his network, and making frequent trips to nearby towns and cities to meet with legislators to submit requests for developmental works. To supplement his income, he decided to establish a rice mill, a move that would not only contribute to his family's prosperity but also elevate his standing in the community. All this happened in just two years after Aditya's birth.

Simultaneously, he also sponsored a group led by his dear friend Vikram for treasure hunting.

One significant milestone in Raghava's journey was when he invited a Member of the Legislative Assembly to inaugurate his rice mill. This move not only garnered attention but also set the stage for Raghava's eventual rise to power within the village. His reputation as a learned man, his sociable nature, and the steady income generated from his land and rice mill made him a well-known figure not only in his own village but also in the surrounding.

All these transformative events in Raghava's life were intrinsically tied to the birth of his son, Aditya. The arrival of this precious child had a profound impact on Raghava, motivating him to strive for success, become an active participant in the political arena, and engage in the wider world outside his village. Amidst his busy schedule, with his hands in various pursuits, Raghava never neglected his duties as a father. Each night, he would lovingly cradle Aditya, caressing him until he drifted into peaceful slumber. His immense love for Aditya remained unwavering.

Indeed, as the years passed and Aditya grew, Raghava's life continued to prosper. At bedtime, Aditya's attachment to his father was even more evident. He would nestle himself in Raghava's strong arms, and as Raghava gently cradled him, Aditya would drift off to sleep, feeling safe and loved. His father's rhythmic breathing and the soothing sound of his heartbeat were the lullaby that comforted Aditya each night.

There were nights when Aditya would wake up in the middle of his slumber, perhaps from a bad dream or a sudden noise. When that happened, his immediate response was to cry out for his father. Raghava, who was always alert to his son's needs, would rush to Aditya's side. With tender care, he would lift the crying child into his arms and rock him back to sleep. Aditya's sobs would gradually turn into soft whimpers, and then into peaceful silence, as he listened to his father's soothing whispers and felt the gentle caress of his father's hand stroking his hair.

As Raghava's influence and standing in the village continued to grow, many villagers began to see him as a natural candidate for the position of sarpanch in the elections which were held in the year 1983. His dedication to the community, his successful ventures, and his commitment to enhancing village life made him a popular choice among the residents.

One day, a group of villagers approached Raghava, earnestly encouraging him to consider running for the sarpanch position in the upcoming election. They believed that his leadership and vision could bring even greater progress and prosperity to their community.

However, Raghava, despite the villagers' encouragement and support, held a deep sense of respect and admiration for Chinnappa, who had openly expressed his desire to become the sarpanch. Chinnappa, an elderly member of the village, possessed extensive networking skills and had been actively seeking the position for some time. Most believed that Chinnappa was motivated not by selflessness but by a strong fascination with the title and designation of sarpanch - the chair of Sarpanch is what he wanted.

While Raghava acknowledged the villagers' trust and faith in him, he also recognized that challenging Chinnappa for the position would involve more than just a political competition—it would show utter and intended disrespect to Chinnappa and Raghava's character would not suit to such insult to an elderly person who had been communicating his contest for more than five years. Raghava's loyalty to Chinnappa, coupled with his belief that the elder leader still had much to offer the community, weighed heavily on his decision.

In a sincere conversation with the villagers, Raghava expressed his heartfelt gratitude for their support. However, he humbly declined their request to run for the sarpanch position, explaining that he believed Chinnappa's experience and networking abilities could potentially benefit the village.

Instead, Raghava pledged his full support to Chinnappa's candidacy, promising to assist him in any way possible to ensure the village's continued progress and well-being. His decision was met with understanding and appreciation from the villagers, who admired his integrity and commitment to maintaining unity and harmony in the community.

For Raghava, somehow, the memory of the sacrifice of the twenty one soldiers had been etched into his heart since childhood. It could be through his mother's stories, Raghava learned about the soldiers' courage, their determination to protect the treasure, and their willingness to make the ultimate sacrifice. He came to understand the significance of their mission and the profound impact it had on the entire kingdom.

As he grew older, Raghava's determination to honor the memory of the twenty one soldiers only deepened. He resolved to ensure that their sacrifice was never forgotten, that their bravery continued to inspire generations to come.

In the face of revisionist narratives and distorted versions of history which had been trying to portray the soldiers as traitors and thieves, Raghava remained steadfast in his commitment to preserving the truth. He knew that the sacrifices made by those twenty one soldiers deserved to be remembered and celebrated for the genuine valor they represented, not twisted into a tale of betrayal.

The chain of events, from the tragic loss of Naagam to the revelation of the hidden treasure, the birth of Aditya, and the sudden turn of fortune, had a profound impact on Raghava's perspective on life. These occurrences seemed to be interconnected, each carrying a hidden message or purpose that was gradually unraveling before him. Raghava's heart started longing to the same purpose and it became his part - to ensure the dignity of the soldiers promoted and the efforts to hunt the treasure intensified.

To start with, Raghava envisioned a grand revival of the Shivan's festival, one that would not only commemorate the soldiers' heroism but also educate the younger generation about the sacrifice. He saw it as an opportunity to instill values of courage, selflessness, and unity in the hearts of the people.

With a newfound sense of purpose, Raghava embarked on a journey to fulfill this mission. He used his wealth and influence to organize the festival on a scale never seen before. His passion and dedication were infectious, and soon, the entire village of Jhagaaram rallied behind him.

As the festival gained momentum and attracted people from neighboring villages, Raghava's vision began to materialize. The sacrifices of the soldiers were once again in the spotlight, their memory celebrated with fervor and reverence. It became an annual event that united the community, a testament to the enduring legacy of those who had given their lives for a cause greater than themselves.

Parallel, Raghava went beyond the festival celebrations; he increased financing the expedition to uncover the treasure. Vikram's selection as the leader for his sponsored treasure hunting was not merely based on their friendship; he was renowned for his logical thinking and shared Raghava's fervor for the treasure hunt. After Nagam's demise, it had become customary for every young man to embark on at least ten expeditions into the forest, each spanning approximately a week. The troops approached the story of the treasure and the treasure code from every conceivable angle, yet their efforts merely led to the discovery of snake burrows, ant hills, and ancient rudraksha or Arjuna trees.

Among all the troops, the only creative thoughts that emerged were to search the decaying ant hills or, if not, the oldest rudraksha and Arjuna trees. These creative ideas were kept strictly confidential within their respective groups, and maintaining the secrecy of these strategies was considered the utmost display of integrity. With each troop comprising around eight members, they divided the forest area amongst themselves to dig or explore based on their discretion. The teams meticulously kept records of the areas they had searched, maintaining a map of the forest and the territories they covered. Out of the six active troops involved in this thrilling adventure, no two groups operated together or in close proximity. The troops were dispersed in all directions, taking the centre point as Rishi Pahar Mountain, aiming to cover as much ground as possible.

Initially, for a year Vikram worked with another group as a member. As the youngest member of that troop, Vikram found himself blindly following the instructions of the team leader. However, he couldn't shake off the feeling that the search plan seemed vague and impractical. How could an intelligent person provide a clue that hinted at destroying snake burrows and anthills, and required digging up almost twenty percent of the entire forest merely because those areas were covered by Arjuna trees?

The decoding of the story seemed foolish to Vikram. Vikram attempted to express his doubts and concerns, but nobody seemed willing to listen or consider his perspective. As the key words in the code included Lord Shiva, snake, arrow, across the forest, the decoding resulted in rudraksha trees, anthills or snake burrows and Arjuna trees but incidentally the treasure sport of Nagam had all of these nearby and the main reason is that the forest was filled with these and additionally neem trees, banyan trees.

After embarking on numerous adventurous trips spanning a year, each lasting for more than a week, Vikram joined to lead the troop sponsored by his friend Raghava.

Vikram's extraordinary talent lay in his keen eye for details. From a young age, he had the ability to observe and notice even the smallest nuances that others often missed. This meticulous attention to detail was evident in various aspects of his life, from his studies to his everyday observations. It was this remarkable skill that made him excel in tasks requiring precision and thoroughness, such as decoding intricate puzzles and unraveling complex mysteries. Vikram's ability to delve deep into the finer points of any situation set him apart as a master of detail.

As Raghava shouldered huge tasks, his house became an everyday meeting place where he coordinated treasure hunt and the temple related activities. The house of Raghava had a decent verandah in the front which became a public spot to gather and discuss all the social issues also. Otherwise Raghava and Vikram made the most of this restful spot, meeting every alternate day as part of their longstanding tradition.

On these occasions, Vikram would eagerly update Raghava on his latest reflections about the hidden treasure, sharing his thoughts on new paths and unexplored avenues within the forest, as well as the activities of the various treasure-hunting troops. Occasionally, friends and neighbors would join the duo, enhancing the camaraderie with their presence. But as the hours passed, one by one, these visitors would take their leave, until Vikram was often the last to remain. Throughout these gatherings, Raghava's wife would gracefully attend to their guests, serving refreshing tea that kept the conversations flowing as freely as the evening breeze.

In the immediate aftermath of Naagam's tragic demise, the zeal for treasure hunting ran high among the villagers and various groups embarked on missions to uncover the hidden wealth. The forest buzzed with activity as teams of enthusiastic treasure hunters ventured deep into the wilderness, initially driven by the memory of the sacrificed soldiers and the charm of the long-lost riches. However, as the years went by, the initial fervor began to wane. Many treasure hunting expeditions turned into little more than tourist excursions. Groups of friends and thrill-seekers flocked to the forest, treating it as an adventure playground. These gatherings often featured more fun, parties, and picnics than serious attempts at treasure hunting. The spirit that had once burned so brightly diminished, replaced by a sense of casual exploration.

Sadly, some of the treasure-hunting groups took their reckless behavior to extreme levels. Consumed by their immature pleasure-seeking thoughts, they resorted to hunting and killing the wildlife within the forest.

Amidst this shift in attitude, only one group stood out—the troop led by Vikram and funded by Raghava. Their dedication remained unwavering. Unlike the others, they retained a deep reverence for the soldiers and their mission, viewing treasure hunting as a solemn duty rather than a casual pastime.

By the year 1985, a stark shift had occurred in the dynamics surrounding the Naimisha forest. The once solemn and purpose-driven mission of treasure hunting, initially sparked by the sacrifice of the twenty one soldiers and their commitment to preserving the treasure's legacy, had gradually evolved into something quite different.

The destruction of the forest ecosystem, rampant wildlife hunting, and the overall reckless behavior of some treasure hunting groups had escalated dramatically. These activities had reached a point of ecological crisis, threatening the delicate balance of the forest and its inhabitants. The very environment that had held the hidden treasure for so long was now suffering due to human interference.

In stark contrast to this environmental degradation, the grand celebrations at Rishi Pahar had seen an upsurge. What was once a solemn occasion to honor the soldiers and their sacrifice had transformed into a boisterous and exuberant festivity. The true purpose behind the festival, which was to remember and respect the soldiers and their valor, had lost its significance.

This divergence, where environmental destruction peaked on one hand, and celebratory fervor intensified on the other, marked a critical point in the history. The original objectives and purposes of preserving the treasure's memory and fostering a spirit of unity and sacrifice had taken a backseat. People were now drawn more to the allure of celebrations, fun, and partying.

The transformation in public behavior was largely attributed to Raghava. Many believed that his generous financial contributions to the festival's celebrations, as well as his financial support for Vikram's troop and other individuals, had played a significant role. His philanthropy had inadvertently fueled a culture of extravagance and prolonged festivities.

The constant gossip and private talks about Raghava's actions became too much. Friends and family members started coming to Raghava's house to talk about it. Even their calm evenings on the porch were filled with discussions about how to handle the situation. Raghava and Vikram spent a lot of time trying to figure out what to do.

In the early months of 1986, amid all these a jolt of unexpected news reverberated through the villages in the erstwhile kingdom of Vijetha Mandala. Startling orders from the forest department echoed a stern warning against trespassing into the woods in pursuit of hidden treasures. The announcement of orders from the forest department reached every village. To create awareness, the forest department in association with the police department organized the first meeting in Jhagaaram inviting all the troops that ventured into the forest in search of the treasure.

The announcements utterly disappointed Raghava.

The gathering was held in the premises of the Gram panchayat of Jhagaaram. The look and feel of many Gram panchayats in 1985 was serene due to the landscape filled with huge trees with branches stretching many meters and the roots bulging out from the earth. Except two small rooms with walls made of stones and the roof with teak wood planks, the Gram panchayat had no other ceiling to sit under for big meetings and hence, the gatherings were more under the trees.

That meeting was attended by not only the troops but by many youth who had plans to be a part of the expedition. The verandah of the panchayat rooms acted as the stage for the meeting and the forest officer preceded the meeting and was led by the subordinates. On the stage was the sarpanch, ward members and the two officers from the forest department. The two police who accompanied for security to the forest officers were resting somewhere far from the stage.

'Good morning everyone. We have with us the forest department officer to share the orders against any expedition into the forest to search the treasure.' One of the forest officers started to give the introduction on the purpose of gathering but then he was interrupted by a random person in the crowed.

'We know what we are doing. We are not destroying the forest.'

'We have come with the orders. First listen to the orders if not we can just leave the papers here and leave. We want to explain the orders in detail so that you are extra careful.'

'Who are you to give the orders, this is our village and this is our forest.' Another random voice from the crowd shouted followed by the supporting voices from almost every audience.

'If you do not want to hear, it is easy for us, anyhow our duty is to paste it on the wall of this office and leave.'

'Why don't we listen to them, let's talk later.' Raghava stood up to take the responsibility for the crowd and added, 'You carry on sir, but you have to answer all the questions after reading the order.'

'Yes, I request the officer to share the orders with you.' The officer got up and read the orders.

'Dear Public of Jhagaram block,

This letter serves as an official order, to the Jhagaram block comprising eighteen villages, to immediately halt the ongoing expedition in Naimisha Forest until further notice. The decision has been made to ensure the preservation of our natural ecosystems, protect wildlife, and prevent potential environmental damage.

After a thorough evaluation, the Forest Department has obtained compelling evidence of damages caused by public activities in search of a mythical treasure within the forest area. These activities have resulted in habitat destruction, unauthorized digging, and disturbance to sensitive species, posing a severe threat to the ecological balance.

As the governing body responsible for forest conservation and management, the Forest Department is entrusted with safeguarding the natural resources and biodiversity of our region. This order is issued to protect the fragile ecosystem and prevent further harm caused by the ongoing expedition.

We hereby instruct and demand your immediate compliance with this order. All individuals and groups engaged in the expedition must cease all activities related to it within the area of Naimisha Forest. The Forest Department cautions against the influence of treasure fables, noting a concerning rise in youth venturing into the forest. Citizens are urged to discourage the spread of mythical stories for the preservation of both nature and safety. It is imperative that you understand the gravity of this decision and strictly adhere to the imposed restrictions. Non-compliance will be met with legal consequences and severe environmental penalties.

We sincerely appreciate your understanding, cooperation, and commitment to the conservation efforts of the Forest Department. Together, let us protect our natural heritage and ensure its preservation for the well-being of current and future generations.'

The atmosphere crackled with tension as the officer retreated to his chair. The forceful shout from Raghava had struck a nerve, reverberating through the crowd and piercing the officer's authority.

'How dare you read it here?' Raghava's voice echoed with resentment, filling the air with an undercurrent of rebellion.

'Hold your tongue!' shouted the subordinate, his anger intense as he stepped forward. 'He is the officer, and he has the authority to issue the order. You must show respect.'

Raghava stood his ground, his eyes ablaze with defiance. 'None has the authority to call the treasure mythical,' he retorted, his voice unwavering.

'One mere word shouldn't make you disrespect the officer,' the subordinate persisted, his tone tinged with frustration.

'One mere word?' Raghava jeered, suspicious. 'You mean to say the word is mere. We demand that the word be removed from the order.'

With determination, Raghava advanced towards the stage, the villagers rallying behind him, their voices harmonizing in a chorus of dissent. 'Yes, the word should be removed immediately, and we demand that the orders be quashed!'

The officer, sensing the growing storm of protest, rose to his feet, his voice carrying across the unrestrained crowd. 'This is an order. We will not change it,' he declared, his words met with a wave of angry murmurs. 'Anyone found searching for the treasure will face serious consequences.'

'No order that insults our heroes will be entertained!' proclaimed Vikram, his voice piercing through the commotion as he raised his forefinger defiantly.

'Go back, forest department!' Raghava led the slogans, his rallying cry amplified by the fervor of the gathered villagers. The resounding chorus of 'Go back, go back!' echoed across the village of Jhagaram.

While the chants reverberated through the streets, the officials, undeterred by the mounting unrest, attempted to solidify their orders by pasting them on the walls. But the people, fueled by a collective fury, tore the papers off with determination, their actions serving as an act of defiance against the oppressive regime. Some seized the officers' files and set them ablaze on the roads.

News of the protest spread like wildfire, reaching nearby villages in a matter of moments. It attracted the attention of the media, who rushed to capture the raw intensity of the gathering storm. In less than an hour, an enormous crowd had assembled, swelling with anger and determination, their voices raised in unity against the unjust orders. It was a sight that neither the department nor the protestors had imagined or planned for.

The village of Jhagaaram had become a hotbed of tension and anticipation. The officers had no hint of the uprising that awaited them. They had only two policemen as security, following the standard procedure. Little they know that the gathering of the public in Jhagaaram was far beyond what they had anticipated.

As the officers stood before the surging crowd, their faces reflecting their unease, a voice boomed out from within the masses. 'We cannot leave you people; you will be burnt to death!' A person emerged from the crowd, his eyes filled with anger and frustration. He lunged towards one of the officers, aiming a punch at his face.

Reacting swiftly, one of the police officers intervened. 'Let's go into the room; it's not safe to be out here!' he shouted over the disorder, gesturing towards the gram panchayath room. Recognizing the urgency of the situation, the officers ushered their team towards the gram panchayat room, seeking refuge from the brewing storm.

However, just as they entered the room, the Sarpanch of the village swiftly locked the door from the outside, effectively imprisoning the officials. The action sent a powerful message—arresting the very people who were meant to uphold law and order.

Word of this unprecedented event quickly spread throughout the surrounding villages, carried by messengers and whispers. The news reached the nearby police station, stirring them from their routine. The public from all the neighboring villages began streaming towards Jhagaaram, driven by both curiosity and solidarity. The police, realizing the magnitude of the situation, promptly called upon reinforcements from their station and nearby stations, mobilizing all available personnel.

Outside the gram panchayat room, the atmosphere was electric. The sprawling space around the building was dotted with tamarind and neem trees, their branches offering shelter from the scorching sun. People gathered in small groups, engaging in animated conversations based on their level of acquaintance. The topic that dominated their discussions was the 'mythical treasure,' a term that had intrigued and captivated their imaginations.

Among the groups, a new theory emerged, spreading like wildfire. It was proposed that the use of the term 'mythical treasure' was a deliberate ploy by the royal family, an elaborate conspiracy aimed at deceiving the villagers. The logic behind this theory resonated with many, and the message quickly spread from one group to another. Soon, a unanimous agreement formed among the villagers, fueling their resolve to stand against any injustice perpetrated by the authorities.

As the tension mounted, the officers locked inside the room could only imagine the magnitude of the gathering outside. They were now fully aware that their earlier underestimation had put them in a dangerous position.

As the village heads and key individuals gathered under the shade of the trees, their faces etched with concern, they knew that a united strategy was necessary to secure the release of the imprisoned officers. Voices were raised, ideas were exchanged, and a plan gradually took shape.

It was unanimously decided that all available village heads would form a delegation and seek the intervention of the local Member of Legislative Assembly (MLA). The MLA held the power to influence higher authorities and could potentially defuse the volatile situation in Jhagaaram. With their course of action decided, the group of village heads set off to meet the MLA, hiring a jeep.

Meanwhile, among the crowd, a smaller group started to form around Raghava, consisting of youngsters, treasure hunters, and a few descendants of the twenty-one soldiers. Raghava possessed a charisma that attracted people to him. His voice resonated with conviction, his pace carried a sense of urgency, and his logic was persuasive.

Addressing the gathering, Raghava's voice carried over the murmurs of the crowd. 'Listen, my friends. Many police personnel will undoubtedly arrive to protect the locked officers, but we must try to delay them from opening the door. We must make the government understand the gravity of this situation. How dare anyone label our treasure as mythical? It is the conspiracies of the shameless royal family! We must not stand for it!'

His words ignited a fire within the hearts of those who listened. Determination excelled in their eyes as they vowed to stand united against injustice. The villagers knew that this was not merely a struggle for the officers' freedom; it was a battle to reclaim their heritage, their pride, and their rightful place in history.

As the minutes ticked by, tensions continued to mount. The villagers awaited the return of the delegation meeting with the MLA, hoping for a positive outcome. But deep down, they understood that their fight was far from over. They were prepared to face any challenge that came their way, for the spirit of unity and defiance now coursed through their veins, driving them forward with unwavering resolve.

Within the span of few hours, a flurry of events unfolded in Jhagaaram. The additional police personnel, accompanied by the village heads who had gone to meet the MLA, arrived at the gram panchayat. With a sense of urgency, the village heads relayed the outcome of their meeting with the MLA. Due to prior commitments, the MLA could not come immediately to Jhagaaram, but he assured them that within a week, he would arrange a meeting with the forest department officials responsible for the order. While it wasn't the immediate resolution they had hoped for, the villagers found solace in the fact that their concerns were acknowledged, and a path towards a solution had been set.

Guided by the MLA's instructions, the villagers made the difficult decision to release the officers from the room. It was a gesture of goodwill, demonstrating their commitment to resolving the conflict through dialogue rather than through confrontation. The locked door swung open, and the officers emerged, their expressions a mix of relief and apprehension.

As the officers stepped out into the open, the atmosphere in Jhagaaram underwent a subtle shift. The crowd, though still resolute, held a glimmer of hope for a peaceful resolution. They recognized that their battle was not against individual officers but against a system that had marginalized and dismissed their heritage.

While their immediate objective had been achieved, the villagers understood that their struggle was far from over. The upcoming meeting with the MLA would be crucial. But for now, they stood united, eager to take the next steps on their journey towards reclaiming their treasure and restoring justice to the sacrifice of the soldiers.

As promised, the MLA gave the appointment to the people who wanted to discuss the issue. As it needed to travel nearly fifty kilometers to meet the MLA, only limited people had to go, Chinnappa who was the Sarpanch of Jhagaram, had taken lead to take the consent of as many leaders as possible to sort out the list of people who would be attending the meeting. It included Sarpanches of 18 villages, leaders of treasure hunting troops, educated people, and prominent heirs of the soldier's family and Raghava was undoubtedly in the list. Raghava, in fact was in the decision making along with the Sarpanch to finalize the list, hence influenced to include Vikram in the list. After the list was finalized, Raghava was the natural choice to take care of the arrangements.

At the party office:

The newly constructed party office in the district headquarters provided the setting for the important meeting. The journey to reach the venue had been long, starting before sunrise and continuing until afternoon. For many of the attendees, it was their first visit to the bustling city. As they parked their bullock carts outside the office compound, a staff member warmly welcomed them and invited them to enjoy a complimentary lunch at the canteen. The gesture brought smiles to the faces of the visitors, appreciating the thoughtful hospitality displayed by the party.

'Sir is on a field visit, please gather in the main hall after lunch. You don't need to worry about paying anything in the canteen; it's taken care of by the sir,' the staff member informed them before departing.

The presence of the MLA was immediately noticed as the attendees hurriedly finished their lunches and made their way to the main hall. The space was grand, capable of accommodating a thousand people, with wooden frames that could be used to partition the hall for multiple events simultaneously.

The MLA, known for his wise understanding of human dynamics and his ability to connect with different audiences, had strategically chosen the circular seating arrangement for the meeting. This was one of the many tricks up his sleeve to create the desired atmosphere and set the tone for effective communication.

When dealing with voters or constituents, especially in situations where extensive discussions and dialogue were expected, the MLA often preferred a circular seating arrangement without any tables. This arrangement communicated trust among the audience and they would speak their heart out. The MLA had no special chair, got mingled with the attendees in the first circle.

The first circle had the MPTC, Chinnappa, Raghava and the immediate family members of the soldiers.

'Sarpanch sir, how are you? Namaste, everyone,' greeted the MLA, introducing himself to the visitors with a sense of warmth and familiarity.

'Namaste, sir. We are all well, thanks to your support,' responded the attendees, rising from their seats to extend their wishes to the MLA.

'How are our schemes progressing in your villages?' inquired the MLA, eager to gauge the impact of the government initiatives.

'The ration distribution is going smoothly, sir. However, we are in need of more housing facilities. Overall, the people are responding positively to the government's efforts.' spoke one of the attendees.

'Thank you for your feedback. We are working to secure more approvals for housing schemes, but unfortunately, a significant portion of the state quota has been allocated to cities and towns. I assure you that I will consider your applications,' assured the MLA, acknowledging the need for further development.

'We have complete faith in you, sir. Always,' affirmed another attendee, their sentiment echoed by the chorus of agreement from the rest of the gathering.

'Ah, now tell me, what is the matter with the forest department?' the MLA inquired, shifting the focus to the pressing issue at hand.

'Sir, we are aware of the royal family's efforts to halt the treasure-hunting activities, but it was a surprise to learn that the forest department is supporting their cause. They have issued orders to cease all treasure hunting and have even labeled the treasure as mythical,' explained one of the attendees.

'Mythical treasure? Is that what they called it?' the MLA sought clarification, his brows furrowing in concern.

'Yes, sir. It was mentioned in the orders. However, we have been engaged in treasure hunting for decades, and two treasures have been discovered till now. Unfortunately, all the evidence was lost due to personal influence from the royal family,' lamented the attendee, expressing the frustration caused by the suppression of their findings.

The MLA, concerned and eager to understand the situation in detail, turned to the assistant collector and requested a thorough explanation of what had transpired. The assistant collector, aware of the gravity of the matter, began recounting the events to shed light on the actions of the forest department.

'The forest department received a complaint attached with recorded videos and photographs showcasing the treasure hunting activities. This evidence depicted snake burrows that were dug, anthills disturbed, pits excavated, trees cut down, and unfortunate instances of animals being killed in the process and many seen partying and camping.' the assistant collector began, painting a vivid picture of the environmental impact caused by the treasure hunting.

'Upon receiving these alarming reports, the forest department felt compelled to respond swiftly. Before taking any action, however, they conducted a comprehensive inquiry within the village itself. Numerous individuals were interviewed, and it was disheartening to discover that many of them admitted to engaging in the activities detailed in the presented proofs,' continued the assistant collector, the weight of disappointment evident in his voice.

'The villagers themselves, during the inquiry, were questioned about the treasure and the story surrounding it. To our dismay, a significant number of them expressed the belief that the treasure was nothing more than a myth. They in fact claimed that the soldiers were traitors and that they were killed by the king.' the assistant collector explained.

The assistant collector's account portrayed a complex situation. On one hand, the forest department had undeniable evidence of the environmental damage caused by the treasure hunting activities. On the other hand, the villagers themselves seemed to question the authenticity of the treasure and the historical narrative attached to it. This divergence in perspectives added further layers of complexity to the issue at hand, leaving the MLA to consider the course of action that needed to be taken against the complaint received.

The conversation in the meeting room continued, with the participants engaging in a lively discussion. The MLA sought to clarify the origins of the complaint, prompting the assistant collector to respond.

'But who complained?' inquired the MLA, his curiosity piqued.

'It was Mr. Karunakar and Ankaram, sir. They were the ones who brought the matter to the attention of the forest department,' answered the assistant collector, providing the requested information.

Raghava, unable to contain himself, rose from his seat and spoke up with determination. 'There are some among us who hold direct ties to the royal family. We cannot solely rely on their perspective in considering this matter,' he declared boldly, his voice carrying a hint of defiance.

The assistant collector responded calmly. 'We are a republic country, and we are bound by rules. Every individual has the right to lodge a complaint and to protect the environment,' he explained, emphasizing the need to address concerns without prejudice.

Raghava countered, highlighting an important aspect that went beyond the immediate complaint. 'But what about the legend that states the existence of the treasure? Who will delve into the past and unravel the intricacies of the story? It is crucial to visit all the villages, listen to the legends surrounding the treasure, and then make an informed decision. The villages and the people that were visited by the forest department is evidently fighting for the prestige of the royal family. This bias is well-known among the people,' he argued, presenting a case for the exploration of diverse perspectives.

The room fell into a momentary silence, the participants absorbing Raghava's impassioned words.

'And Sir, I think the debate had now shifted from the immediate complaint on environmental implications to the larger narrative surrounding the treasure. The question of historical authenticity and the need for a comprehensive understanding of the legend had been raised. We think there should be no debate on the sacrifice of the soldiers, people who saw their cruel death still live.' Raghava concluded.

'Mr. Additional collector, does the forest department have any rights to call the treasure mythical? How come are they eligible to speak on history?' Asked the MLA.

'Yes sir, the Forest Department can help debunk superstitions and foster a greater appreciation for the natural world based on scientific understanding. Education and awareness initiatives can be effective in dispelling myths, misconceptions, and superstitions related to forests, wildlife, and natural resources.'

'But they cannot dismiss the history.' Argued the MLA.

'Sir, yes but there is no concrete evidence against the claim that the soldiers have sacrificed.' Replied the Additional collector.

'Do the forest officers have the power to issue orders without the consent from the district administration?'

'Sir, yes, they have the power but they have to CC to the collector, which has happened.'

'Ok, so everything has happened as per the process, so how to resolve the issue.' Asked the MLA.

'Sir, the orders are strict and you know about the collector and the range officer, they are stringent. We have to request the villagers to resist from any such activities.' Replied the assistant collector.

'What do you demand, Chinnappa' Asked the MLA to the Sarpanch of Jhagaram.

'We demand to take back the orders.'

'Additional collector sir, can the orders given by the forest department be taken back.'

' Yes sir, the issued orders can be withdrawn under compelling situations but need to be backed by the evidence or in case the orders give rise to unintended consequences.'

'So please inform the range officer that we shall have a meeting with the collector soon.' MLA continued shifting his looks to the visitors and said, 'Look the district collector is on vacation, he might be back in the office in a week. As soon as he comes back, we shall have a meeting. I shall invite four to five among you also to come to the meeting. I will inform you.'

'Thank you so much sir, we are grateful to you forever.' Said Chinnappa.

'Everything will set right, but till then, request your people not to venture into the forest.' Said the MLA.

After the discussion on the issue, the sarpanch submitted various requests, files related to their constituency and every dispersed.

Four weeks had passed since the last meeting with the MLA and the other officers, yet there had been no word or updates from any of them. The villagers had diligently adhered to the MLA's instructions, refraining from engaging in any activities that could be deemed as unforeseen. However, as time went on, their patience began to wane, and they felt the need to seek further answers. It was then that news reached them: the MLA himself would soon be visiting their village.

The meeting was scheduled to take place at the house of Chinnappa. A strict directive was issued, allowing only those who had visited the MLA in town to attend the meeting. In an effort to maintain order and exclusivity, it was emphasized that people from other villages should not enter Jhagaram.

It was the first time that an MLA was visiting a house in that village for a purpose. The preparations for the meeting were meticulously carried out. The chairs were arranged in the backyard, sheltered under a cloth tent. The food was carefully prepared, taking into account the specific preferences of the MLA. Attention was paid to every detail, ensuring that tea, water, and other necessities were readily available.

Everyone expected the entry of the MLA would be at noon but the white ambassador car arrived surprisingly in the morning, around 10 o'clock. Despite its punctuality, the participants were already gathered at the meeting place. Chinnappa and Raghava promptly approached the car, extending a respectful greeting to the MLA.

'Sir, Namaste,' he said, bowing slightly as a sign of respect. They then invited the MLA to his house, where he introduced his family. As a gesture of hospitality, a glass of water and a cup of tea were offered to the MLA before they made their way to the meeting venue.

To the villagers' surprise, the MLA arrived alone, without any accompanying bureaucrats such as the district collector or additional collector. Only two security personnel accompanied him, a notable departure from the usual staff that would accompany him on his visits. It was a simple visit, uncharacteristic of the grand displays of power and authority that typically accompanied the MLA's movements. Absent were the additional ambassador cars, police jeeps, and motorcycles that usually formed a convoy around him.

This unexpected simplicity in the MLA's arrival increased the curiosity of the villagers, leaving them intrigued about the purpose and nature of this particular visit. As they awaited the commencement of the meeting, anticipation and questions filled the air, leaving the participants eager to hear what the MLA had to say and hoping to find answers to their concerns.

The atmosphere in Chinnappa's house was heavy with anticipation and a sense of disillusionment. The gathered villagers looked expectantly at the MLA, hoping for a glimmer of hope.

'I must seek your apologies first,' the MLA began, his voice unusually low and filled with a hint of defeat. The room fell into silence, everyone eager to hear what he had to say.

'I thought it was a simple issue, but both the head of our party and the head of the government are silent on the orders,' the MLA continued, his words carrying a weight that resonated through the room. The villagers exchanged glances, their disbelief evident on their faces.

'But why are they so stringent on this?' Chinnappa's voice trembled with a mix of anger and frustration. 'Are they aware of the real struggle our land has undergone? Are they aware of the sacrifice of the soldiers?'

The MLA sighed and a deep weariness etched on his face. 'Believe me, Chinnappa, I have met our party president and the chief minister exclusively on this issue. They asked me to leave the issue and that nothing can be done against the orders. And they are very much aware of the issue. I stayed in the capital city for four days only for this, but it was all in vain.'

The room buzzed with a mix of disbelief and disappointment. The realization that even their own leaders had turned a blind eye to their cause sent shockwaves through the villagers' hearts.

Chinnappa went numb and no one dared to raise their voice but then came Raghava's voice, 'They are under the influence, no doubt,' Raghava declared, his voice tinged with anger, and he continued 'Who can influence the chief minister?'

Random voices emerged in a single tone saying 'the royal family, who else then?'

For a moment, the room fell into a heavy silence as the gravity of the situation sank in. The villagers exchanged glances, their hopes diminishing, but understanding that the obstacles before them were far greater than they had imagined.

'I am very sorry, Chinnappa. I am helpless, but I have tried my best for you all,' the MLA expressed, his voice filled with remorse.

'You have done your best, sir. We understand,' Chinnappa assured him, his voice carrying a hint of resignation. 'But it's not in your hands.'

Raghava, driven by a determination to fight for what was right, couldn't let the conversation end on such a disheartening note. 'But how do we go further?' he asked, his eyes searching for any glimmer of a solution.

The room fell into a contemplative silence, the weight of their struggle hanging heavily in the air. The journey ahead seemed daunting, their path filled with seemingly impossible obstacles.

'Unexpected. We had no apprehensions after we met you at your party office. The issue is a smaller one for you, we thought, it would be solved with no obstacles.' It was only Raghava who was on the questioning side while Chinnappa couldn't voice his concern and all others could only give chorus to what Raghava said.

'Yes, we thought the orders would be dismissed, and it's only a matter of time,' Vikram and the other there lamented, their voice filled with disappointment.

'We don't know what more can be done. The state is against us,' another villager added, their tone tinged with a sense of hopelessness.

'I am deeply saddened by the response from my leadership. This issue may seem trivial to them, but for us, it is a matter of our existence' the MLA interjected, his voice heavy with regret.

'It is not trivial, sir. If our leadership is so adamant about these orders and refuses to engage in any discussion, then it is clear that there is a larger conspiracy at play,' Raghava spoke up, his words resonating with conviction.

'Conspiracy?' echoed the villagers, by the mere mention of the word.

'Yes, there is a possibility that the leadership of your party has been influenced by the royal family,' Raghava explained, his voice unwavering.

'But none of the members of the royal family reside here. Why would they do such a thing?' someone questioned, seeking clarity.

'The royal family needs to maintain their reputation and influence,' Raghava replied. 'Raghava, let's not make baseless assumptions,' Chinnappa cautioned, a hint of concern in his voice.

Raghava, undeterred, continued, 'Think about it. Why would the government be so stringent and concerned about such a small issue when our state is grappling with countless other pressing problems?'

The room fell into silence as Raghava's words hung in the air, stirring thoughts and suspicions.

The MLA, realizing his inability to provide a solution, stood up, signaling his departure. 'Raghava, Chinnappa, dear representatives, I apologize for my helplessness. I must take my leave,' he expressed with a tinge of sadness.

Chinnappa, in a gesture of hospitality, approached the MLA to invite him for lunch, but he politely declined, feeling disheartened by the turn of events.

The villagers exchanged glances, their hearts heavy with the realization that their fight had become more complicated than they initially thought. Yet, beneath the surface of disappointment and uncertainty, a spark of determination flickered within each of them, fueling their resolve to uncover the truth and fight for their cultural identity and the symbol of sacrifice that meant so much to their community.

The villages buzzed with discussions and fervent conversations as people gathered in small groups, united by their shared desire to honor the sacrifice of the soldiers and reclaim their rights. They contemplated on how best to proceed with their protest, aiming to challenge the order that dismissed their heritage as mere myth and claimed the treasure to be off-limits.

In this sea of passionate voices, each group sought to convey their sentiments to Raghava, recognizing him as a representative who could effectively communicate their emotions. One after another, leaders of the various small groups approached Raghava, sharing their plans of action and seeking his guidance.

As the messages poured in, Raghava found himself consumed by his responsibility to organize and channel the collective will of his people. Meetings with youth from different neighborhoods, as well as established political groups, filled his schedule from morning to night. Vikram, loyal to Raghava, dutifully attended to the tasks assigned to him, further strengthening the coordination within their team.

Together, they became the sought-after leaders, guiding the collective effort towards their shared goal.

In this process, somewhere Chinnappa felt he was neglected by the masses as the influence of Raghava grew but Chinnappa too started being aggressive in fueling and sustaining the anger.

Numerous suggestions poured in from the passionate villagers, each group proposing their strategies for protest and resistance. Recognizing the need to keep track of these valuable contributions, Raghava took on the responsibility of documenting the meetings, diligently recording the ideas put forth by each group. The house of Raghava transformed into a hub of collaboration and discussion, with people flocking to share their suggestions and contribute to the cause.

After carefully seeking suggestions from a diverse range of volunteer groups, individuals, learned individuals, politically active individuals, and various other organizations, a comprehensive plan began to take shape. The goal was to initiate a statewide movement named 'Shivan's Pride' that would aim to restore the glory of Shivans and reclaim the rights to search for the treasure in the forest.

To effectively tackle this mission, three distinct branches were established, each with its own role and responsibilities. These branches were known as the Guardians, the Hunters, and the Activists. Each branch had a specific focus and target audience, working collaboratively to achieve the overarching objective.

The Guardians took on the vital role of connecting with the general public and raising awareness about the significance of Shivan's tale. In the form of dramas, songs and stage shows, they passionately shared the stories, legends, and folklore surrounding the treasure, aiming to garner widespread support from the common people. The Guardians acted as ambassadors, encouraging individuals to join the cause, attend rallies, and participate in peaceful demonstrations. Their role was to build a strong foundation of public support for the movement.

On the other hand, the Hunters, fueled by their unwavering determination, delved into the depths of the forest in search of the elusive treasure. As there was the arrest warrant against the intruders into forest, the Hunters operated in secret. Equipped with their knowledge, expertise, and a deep connection to the land, they ventured into the wilderness, meticulously scouring every corner for any trace of the hidden wealth. The Hunters were driven by the belief that uncovering the treasure would not only reclaim their cultural identity but also symbolize the triumph of sacrifice and perseverance.

Simultaneously, the Activists took on the critical task of engaging with politicians, bureaucrats, lawyers, and other influential figures. They utilized their persuasive skills, knowledge of the legal system, and network of contacts to rally support from those in positions of power. The Activists tirelessly lobbied for policy changes, advocated for the rights of the people, and sought alliances with like-minded organizations. Their primary aim was to create a favorable environment for the movement, ensuring that the concerns of the community were heard and addressed at higher levels.

Through the combined efforts of the Guardians, Hunters, and Activists, the 'Shivan's Pride' movement gained momentum. The diverse skill sets, resources, and strategies of each branch complemented one another, forming a strong and united front. The campaign resonated with people from all walks of life, igniting a sense of pride and determination within the hearts of those who believed in the significance of Shivan's tale.

As the movement gained traction, the branches continued to collaborate, sharing updates, experiences, and insights. Regular meetings were held to synchronize efforts, discuss progress, and refine strategies.

The 'Shivan's Pride' movement became a beacon of hope, uniting individuals from various backgrounds under a common cause. It captured the attention of the entire state, sparking conversations, inspiring others to stand up for their cultural heritage, and bringing the issue to the forefront of public consciousness.

With the Guardians spreading the word, the Hunters exploring the depths of the forest, and the Activists advocating for change, the movement surged forward with determination. The journey ahead was filled with uncertainties, but the collective spirit of the Guardians, Hunters, and Activists propelled them forward, firmly believing in their ability to restore Shivan's legacy and reclaim what was rightfully theirs.

Word of the movement quickly spread throughout the state, capturing the attention of not only the common people but also those in influential political circles. As the momentum grew, so did the pressure to address and respond to the demands of the movement. The forest department and the police force were reinforced with paramilitary personnel to prevent the hunters from entering the forest. Despite the increased security measures and numerous arrests, the resolve of the hunters remained unshaken.

'We are a population of over twenty five thousand strong. Do you really think your prisons can contain us all?' Raghava's powerful slogan reverberated through the hearts of the impassioned youth, fueling their determination to fight for their cause. The youth, driven by their unwavering conviction, grew increasingly defiant and fearless in the face of adversity.

Days turned into weeks, and the tension escalated as the chief of police personally visited the villages to deliver a chilling message. He announced that starting the following month, anyone found in the forest would be subject to shoot-on-sight orders. It was an unprecedented curfew-like situation imposed upon the forest, with only the forest dwellers being granted special identity cards to access their ancestral lands. The message struck a chord of fear and anger within the hearts of the people, further fueling their determination to fight for their rights.

The collective anger and determination reached its pinnacle, culminating in one of the largest protests the district had witnessed.

Raghava, Vikram, and a few close associates of them, driven by his unwavering commitment to the cause, embarked on a hunger strike in the district headquarter, setting an example for others to follow. Chinnappa too joined the hunger strike on the same stage after a day.

Two hundred bullock carts, brimming with passionate individuals from the surrounding villages, rallied towards the district headquarter, their determined footsteps echoing the resounding call for justice. The villages were virtually emptied as almost every person either joined the bullock cart procession or stood united at the site of the hunger strike.

The revolution had reached its zenith, its significance echoing far beyond the boundaries of the district. The politicians and Bureaucrats too, recognizing the gravity of the situation, made a plea to call off the strike and rallies. However, the intensity of the movement had surpassed the control of any individual or authority. The people's resolve remained unyielding, their unified voice demanding justice and the restoration of their rights.

Despite many attempts by others to dissuade the hunger fast, they remained steadfast. However, when Prakash Devan intervened on the third day and approached Chinnappa on the stage, he agreed to halt the strike after receiving assurance that Prakash Devan would facilitate negotiations with the government. When the designated leader, Chinnappa ended the strike, it was official to the crowd that the hunger strike ended. With no other option, Raghava and others were compelled to end his strike as well though they were not convinced with Prakash Devan.

Prakash Devan was a renowned activist, a land lord and was the chairman of many aided colleges. He was widely respected for his unwavering commitment to social causes. His aided college stood as a beacon of inclusive education, welcoming students from all backgrounds. As an activist, he passionately championed various movements from environmental conservation, and education to women's rights. Prakash Devan's dedication to social justice and ability to mobilize people made him a remarkable figure in the community.

Relief washed over the faces of the onlookers, and Prakash Devan breathed a sigh of relief himself. He then motioned towards the crowd and said, 'everyone, please understand that this is a crucial step for us to proceed more constructively. Let's come together and work towards our shared goal.'

As Prakash Devan handed Chinnappa a glass of lemon water, symbolizing the conclusion of the hunger strike, the crowd erupted in applause and expressions of gratitude. Prakash Devan turned to Chinnappa and said, 'Now, let me talk to the central minister. Together, we will find a way to bring justice to Shivan's tale and restore its rightful place.'

As news of the Shivan's Pride movement spread beyond the borders of the state, it caught the attention of some international news outlets. Sensationalized headlines and stories began to circulate, painting a negative image of India and its people. The narrative portrayed Indians as backward, superstitious individuals who were willing to destroy their forests in a fruitless search for a mythical treasure.

International newspapers picked up on the protests and the government's efforts to contain the movement, presenting it as a clash between traditional beliefs and progress. The articles highlighted the supposed irrationality of the Indian people, questioning their intelligence and judgment.

Headlines such as '**Indians Seek Treasure in Fairy Tales, Ignoring Environmental Consequences**' '**Superstition vs. Conservation: India's Dilemma**' and '**Mythical Treasure, consuming Forests - a Fable's Pleasure**' adorned the front pages, further reinforcing the negative perception. The stories were filled with descriptions of forest destruction, misguided beliefs, and a lack of scientific understanding.

The portrayal deeply troubled many Indians, who felt that their rich cultural heritage was being reduced to mere superstition and ignorance.

As news of the Shivan's Pride movement reached the international media, it sparked a divisive response among different factions within India. While some environmental activists recognized the importance of preserving cultural heritage and saw the movement as a means to raise awareness about the ecological value of forests, others vehemently opposed what they deemed as promoting superstitions and damaging environmental practices.

A segment of environmental activists aligned themselves with the international media's portrayal, viewing the Shivan's Pride movement as an example of regressive beliefs and harmful practices. They argued that the search for a mythical treasure in the forests was a misguided endeavor that undermined the importance of scientific conservation efforts and perpetuated destructive behaviors. These activists called for a focus on evidence-based approaches and criticized the movement for diverting attention and resources away from pressing environmental issues.

On the other hand, supporters of the Shivan's Pride movement, including cultural enthusiasts, historians, and local communities, saw the movement as an opportunity to reconnect with their roots and preserve their cultural identity. They emphasized that the movement went beyond mere superstitions and instead sought to honor the historical significance of Shivan's tale while advocating for responsible and sustainable practices in the forests.

As pledged, Prakash Devan orchestrated a meeting between the resolute Shivan activists and the team of minister of environment that included the personal secretary to the minister, forest department officials, and a few other officers. The venue for this pivotal meeting was a humble office, adorned with unassuming wooden furnishings that mirrored the practicality of the times. Adorning the walls were framed portraits of national leaders, instilling a sense of patriotism and purpose.

Soft, filtered sunlight streamed through delicate lace curtains, casting a warm and inviting ambiance upon the well-worn carpeted floor. Beyond the office's threshold, a small assembly of media representatives gathered in anticipation of updates from the negotiations. Armed with notepads and pencils, these journalists anxiously awaited the outcome of the discussions.

Inside the office, Raghava, Chinnappa, a few more leaders in the movement and Prakash Devan sat across the long rectangular table along with the team from the Ministry of Environment. The atmosphere was charged with anticipation, and the voices of the participants echoed within the walls.

As the officers started to lecture the Shivan's team, it was evident that they were convincing to just call off all the searching for treasure and withdraw the movement citing the India's image internationally. They pushed forward the newspaper clippings for everyone to see.

Raghava, his weathered face revealing years of struggle, expressed his unwavering dedication to the movement. 'We cannot compromise on our mission to restore Shivan's glory.

The treasure hunting should be open to all, without any restrictions,' he asserted firmly.

The personal secretary to the minister, in his calm demeanor contrasting Raghava's intensity, intervened, 'I understand your passion, Raghava, but we must also consider the impact on our environment. We need a balanced approach that respects our cultural heritage and the need to protect our forests.'

The forest department official leaned forward, emphasizing the government's responsibility to conserve natural resources. 'We share your concerns, gentlemen. We must ensure that the forest ecosystem remains intact. Unregulated treasure hunting could have lasting consequences for our environment.'

Chinnappa frowned, initially resistant to any conditions. 'We cannot accept limitations that dilute the essence of our movement,' he stated with conviction.

A senior politician in the minister's team, acting as a mediator and aware of the mounting pressure from the media and environmental activists, interjected, 'Chinnappa, we must consider the bigger picture. The world is watching, and we have an opportunity to showcase our commitment to responsible cultural preservation. Let's find a middle ground.'

'The middle ground would be to allow the treasure hunting for few months. Beyond that, it would be out of my control. Believe me, the pressure from the central government is unbearable,' said the forest officer, directing his words to the minister.

Raghava, growing frustrated, confronted the minister's team, 'Both, the state and the central Governments support each other politically. You cannot take two sides. Are you with us or are you with the royal family?'

The forest officer retorted, 'If we are listening to you, it doesn't mean we are scared of you. You are talking to a public representative.'

Chinnappa, undeterred, asserted his authority, 'He is our representative, and we are talking to him with the right we have. You better remember I am also representing my people. They know the history, and you do not. Hence, we talk to him in such a tone, and he knows the issue deserves such a tone.'

The forest officer, sensing the deadlock, offered a compromise, 'Up to your decision, sir. As I said, my suggestion is to extend the treasure hunting for few more months, three or four. This is the best amicable solution. If it is not agreed upon, then they won't even get one chance to step into the forest. The new technology we are going to adapt will make it easier to find out those who are venturing into the forest.'

Interrupting the officer's speech, the minister addressed Chinnappa directly, 'Chinnappa, the government has to balance many things. You suggest a solution, and we shall look into whether it is practically feasible.'

Raghava, determined to prove the existence of the treasure, intervened and voiced his concern, 'But sir, do we have to bargain for one more year? It is the moral duty of everyone to prove the treasure existed.'

The minister questioned Chinnappa, 'But everyone in your locality knows the treasure existed and the sacrifice. Why are you pressing the issue so much?'

Realizing the need for a compromise, Raghava made a proposition, 'Okay, we shall not ask for anything under one condition. The orders that state the treasure is a myth should be removed, and the government should celebrate the valor of the sacrifice done by our soldiers. Is it possible?'

The minister hesitated, 'No. That is not at all in the vicinity. You have a set of people who oppose it.'

Raghava, desperate for a resolution, pleaded, 'That is why, leave us to the forest. We promise no trees will be cut, and no harm will be done to the wildlife.'

Recognizing the deadlock, the minister proposed a different approach, 'I think we are going nowhere, Raghava and Chinnappa. I have an idea. We have Prakash Devan here, a learned man. Let us promise that we will listen to what he says.' The minister directed his statement to Chinnappa while Raghava and the others listened attentively.

Before Raghava expressed his reluctance to the proposal, Chinnappa agreed, 'Yes, let us,' sensing that he had no other option but to trust Prakash Devan's judgment. After Chinnappa agreed, Raghava and others had no choice to express their hesitancy.

The secretary turned to Prakash Devan, 'Please take into consideration all the aspects and come to a conclusion. But take some time. Meanwhile, I shall attend a brief meeting in the next room and come back.'

The office was filled with an air of uncertainty as Prakash Devan pondered the weight of his decision, knowing that the fate of the Shivan's Pride movement hung in the balance.

Prakash Devan, feeling the weight of responsibility on his shoulders, sat in deep contemplation as the officers and politicians in the room observed him closely. The silence in the room was profound, as all eyes were fixed on him, waiting for his verdict.

Prakash Devan's face displayed a mix of concentration and determination, his brows furrowed as he mentally sifted through the arguments presented during the debate. He understood the significance of the decision he was about to make, knowing that it could shape the future of the Shivan's Pride movement.

After a few moments, Prakash Devan excused himself, indicating that he needed a break. He stepped out of the office, seeking a moment of solitude to gather his thoughts. As he walked towards the washroom, the weight of the situation hung heavy on his mind, causing his steps to be slow and deliberate.

Inside the washroom, Prakash Devan splashed some cold water on his face, trying to clear his mind and regain focus. He took a few deep breaths, allowing himself a brief moment of relief from the intense atmosphere in the room.

Returning to the office, Prakash Devan noticed a cup of tea waiting for him on the table. Without engaging in conversation or acknowledging anyone in the room, he silently took a sip of the tea, savoring its warmth and allowing it to soothe his frayed nerves.

Despite the officers and politicians present, no one attempted to influence Prakash Devan during this critical moment. They understood the importance of his independence and respected his role as a mediator. They observed him from a distance, recognizing the need to grant him the space and time necessary to arrive at a fair and balanced solution.

Prakash Devan remained immersed in his own thoughts, his gaze focused inward as he weighed the arguments, implications, and consequences. As the minutes ticked by, Prakash Devan's behavior began to change. The lines on his forehead relaxed, and a sense of resolve emanated from his expression. It was evident that he had reached a decision, one that he believed would provide a viable middle ground between the opposing viewpoints.

The room fell into silence as the secretary returned from his meeting. Sensing Prakash Devan's newfound clarity, he approached him cautiously, awaiting his verdict. Prakash Devan, with a composed demeanor, was ready to present his proposed solution, one that aimed to reconcile the aspirations of the Shivan's Pride movement with the need for environmental conservation.

'In the brief association with the Shivan's movement, I felt I belonged to the Shivan's family. I understand the pain of sacrifice. The families that have undergone the stress can only be truly understood by those who have experienced it. Like the families of the soldiers, who had to flee and take refuge at some other place, I too have traveled from place to place on foot, slept by the roadside, and begged for work when I became an orphan at the age of five. Now, when someone attempts to dismiss the soldiers' sacrifice as a myth, it is a shame to hear that. It can never be so. While it is true that over time, many sacrifices become lost and forgotten, this sacrifice cannot be brushed aside so intentionally. There are still direct witnesses who are alive, who saw it all with their own eyes. They witnessed the soldiers struggling for breath, their bodies turning blue, and their hearts ceasing to beat with their final breath. They saw the soldiers' eyes wide open, desperately searching for their families, only to be struck down in that very moment.'

Prakash Devan's words reverberated through the room, carrying an air of both determination and sacrifice. His voice shook with emotion as tears streamed down his cheeks, 'If I were to pass judgment solely as an independent person, considering my thoughts and emotions, I would advocate for unhindered treasure hunting, regardless of the destruction it may cause to the forest or the absence of concern for its wildlife. I hold such profound respect for our heroes, my heroes, that I would gladly surrender my life to their cause,' he declared, his voice filled with unwavering conviction and he continued, ' But keeping in view the objections on both the sides, the attention of International media, I would propose for a two year free hand for treasure hunting and upon the discovery of at least one treasure chest, all the proposals made by the Shivan's Pride team have to be met - one is that the state to celebrate officially the valor of the soldiers and another is to invest in the treasure hunting to find out the remaining chests.'

Team from the Shivan's Pride, taken aback by the unexpected proposition, found themselves at a loss for words. The solution Prakash Devan proposed was far from what they had anticipated. They were expecting for least ten years, but this proposition seemed to veer off that course entirely. Raghava and the three others who accompanied Chinnappa shared their hesitation, their expressions reflecting their uncertainty and reluctance to come to such an agreement.

In response, the personal secretary spoke, his voice carrying a tone of deep respect for Prakash Devan's unwavering commitment. 'My sincerest respect to you, Prakash Devan. Your unwavering passion resonates deeply within us all, and as individuals like you navigate the delicate balance of differing perspectives, we pledge our support in our shared pursuit of truth and justice. Securing permission for even a single year was a strenuous task, and yet you have demanded us double that time. With this extended duration, we have a better chance of making significant progress towards finding a solution. I wholeheartedly take on the responsibility of convincing the central minister to issue the necessary orders,' he assured, his voice resonating with determination.

Chinnappa, his heart heavy with the weight of their collective choices, spoke softly yet resolutely, 'Sometimes, circumstances leave us with no other option. As agreed upon, we must abide by this decision.' Saying so, Chinnappa signed on the agreement and pushed it towards the others in the Shivan's Pride team to sign the agreement. Raghava and others in the team had no option but to sign as they cannot object to Chinnappa and Prakash Devan.

Outside the meeting area, the overwhelming sentiment favored the soldiers and their cause, with the majority of people sympathizing with their sacrifices. However, there remained a small but vocal group of supporters of the royal family who spared no effort in their attempts to deviate, obstruct, and discourage any search for the treasure. They were determined to protect the name and fame of the royal family.

Almost two years went by in a flash, like a quick river current. Now, just a few weeks remained until the deadline. But, unfortunately, no one had managed to find the treasure yet.

The people who supported the royals were celebrating with great enthusiasm, while the Shivan's Pride team was feeling deeply disheartened. The situation had become really intense; they absolutely had to find at least one chest of treasure, or their mission would be a failure. However, it seemed like hope was slipping away from them.

Raghava, typically exhausted after a long day's work, had succumbed to a peaceful slumber on that tranquil February night. The cool breeze flowing in from the open window had cradled him into a deep sleep, promising a night of uninterrupted rest. Hours later, stirred from his slumber, Raghava became aware of a subtle knocking at the door. In the dim light, he heard someone whispering his name. In no much time he realized it was Vikram who was in front of the main door.

As he reluctantly rose from his bed, Aditya, his eight year old son, cried out, sensing his father's departure from his side. With Aditya in his arms, Raghava made his way to the door, his drowsiness still lingering. 'Come in, Vikram. What's going on?' he asked, a touch of curiosity in his voice.

Vikram insisted they stay outside. 'Not inside, let's sit on the verandah. I've got something important to share,' he said, settling down.

Raghava joined him, cradling Aditya in his lap. 'You know what time it is now? Is there an urgent update?' he inquired.

With an eager gleam in his eye, Vikram leaned in and declared, 'I've found it - the treasure.'

Raghava's drowsiness was quickly replaced with astonishment. 'What? Are you serious?' he exclaimed, shaking off his remaining sleep.

Vikram was resolute. 'Yes, Raghava. In fact, there are two brass jars in one spot,' he revealed.

Raghava leaned in closer, 'Are you serious? Where is this spot?'

Vikram leaned closer to share his discovery. 'It's over ten kilometers from Rishi Pahar Mountain. Can we go now?' he asked with a sense of urgency.

'Incredible, Vikram, still can't believe, I doubt if I am asleep' replied Raghava, looking around while Vikram stressed if they could go to the spot immediately.

Raghava hesitated, a mix of astonishment and caution in his voice. 'Yes, we can start now but we shouldn't raise unnecessary doubts. Let's go tomorrow morning. And we mustn't breathe a word of this to anyone, not even the family. Let's secure it first.'

Vikram reassured him, 'I've hidden it safely. No one else can find it – only me.'

Raghava sighed with relief. 'That's fantastic. The government will finally know the worth of Shivan's Pride. What you've done is remarkable, Vikram.'

'But we must be extra cautious. This is our only opportunity. How is it possible that there are two jars in one spot? And first, tell me how you found it,' Raghava inquired.

Vikram explained his discovery, 'I decoded the puzzle in my way, leading me to that very spot. The puzzle's story spoke of

Lord Shiva shooting the snake, the size of a mountain, like an arrow. So, I guessed that all the treasure spots would be in a straight line, each a kilometer apart. From the spot where Nagam found the treasure, I followed that line diligently for years and searched along the way. Today, I spotted the iron ring when it struck the rake, and upon digging, I discovered two jars side by side. I closed it and hurried here.'

Raghava contemplated this in silence, then asked, 'Does anyone else know about this?'

Vikram reassured him, 'No, nobody knows. I haven't shared it with anyone. I came straight here after discovering it.'

'This is just incredible, Vikram. I've always had trust in your abilities, and you've made it,' Raghava praised him.

Vikram humbly replied, 'If it weren't for your support, I wouldn't have ventured on this adventure, Raghava. The credit is yours.'

Raghava's excitement bubbled over. 'The real task now is to prove it to the world. I'm sure the government and all its institutions support the royal family. We need to be cautious and use it to prove the sacrifice of the soldiers.'

'Agreed,' Vikram nodded, and Raghava invited him into the house for a meal.

With Aditya still in his arms, they headed inside. 'Let's discuss everything tomorrow. Now, let's get some good rest. We might not sleep well for some days from tomorrow,' Raghava said as he carried Aditya into the bedroom after Vikram had finished eating.

The following morning, Raghava and Vikram set out into the forest, disguised as if they were headed to town. Aditya, as usual, was dropped off at his school by his father.

After parking their scooter behind the bushes, the two friends trekked deep into the woods, finally reaching the spot where Vikram had discovered the treasure. With no one around, they carefully dug up the treasure jars. The intricate designs on the brass jars were a sight to behold. A long chain attached to the jars held an iron ring on the other side. While one jar's tightly fixed cap remained intact with all its screws, the other jar's cap was loose, with its screws undone.

Curiosity got the better of Raghava, and he decided to open the jar with the loose cap. Inside, they found an incredible amount of gold. Coins, bracelets, chains – even the sight of such an amount of gold was not worthy for a common man. It was a fortune fit for royalty. After examining the gold, they sealed the jar and tightened the screws.

'Vikram, what are your thoughts on our next steps?' Raghava pondered as he sat down beside the brass jar.

Raghava thought for a moment. 'I believe we should reveal one to Prakash Devan and Chinnappa and follow their advice. Meanwhile, we should hide the other somewhere outside the forest, in a place easily accessible for us.'

'So you mean we should keep one a secret?' Vikram sought clarity.

'Yes, let's keep using it when needed for the mission,' Raghava decided.

From that day forward, almost every evening, Raghava and Vikram ventured to the town to meet Prakash Devan and

Chinnappa to chalk out the plan to expose the treasure to the government. However, there came a day when both friends mysteriously disappeared. The entire village was thrown into turmoil, launching an exhaustive search throughout the forest, but their efforts proved fruitless. Only the scooter of Raghava was found along the roadside. As months turned into years, the family of Raghava reluctantly accepted that their household's leader was no longer with them, and the mystery surrounding their disappearance remained unsolved

Revealing the buried fortune

Back to 2008

What Aditya distinctly remembered was the sequence of events that emerged in the days leading up to the demise of his father. He very well remembered that during those last few evenings, before their unexplained disappearance, his father and Vikram would sit on the verandah late into the night, discussing the treasure and their meetings with Prakash Devan and Chinnappa. What surprised Aditya was that Chinnappa and Prakash Devan gave it to the police in writing that they had not met Raghava and Vikram recently and specifically in the week before their disappearance.

However, in a saddening turn of events, a few months later, the police, accompanied by some locals, ransacked Raghava's house. They even dug into the floor, searching for any hidden treasure, but their efforts yielded no results. These occurrences fueled Aditya's determination to uncover the truth behind his father's disappearance.

Years later, as Aditya entered his late teens, around sixteen years of age, and Chinnappa had settled into the isolation of his aging years, Aditya boldly confronted him, determined to uncover the truth about his father's mysterious demise.

'I am well aware that you are harboring a dark secret,' Aditya asserted, his youthful vigor surging like a tidal wave. 'My father met with you daily for a week before his death. Tell me what transpired, or I shall ensure you face dreadful consequences.'

Chinnappa, attempting to maintain his composure, retorted with a touch of arrogance, 'Mind your words, young man. Be cautious of whom you address in this manner. How dare you barge into my home and issue threats?'

But Aditya, his patience worn thin, shot back with scorn, 'your entire political career is owed to my father, yet you choose to conceal the truth, you deceitful old man.'

As this heated exchange unfolded, a growing crowd began to gather, drawn by the escalating confrontation. One concerned onlooker hurried to inform Aditya's mother of the fuss.

Aditya, undeterred by the gathering crowd, continued to scold Chinnappa, accusing him openly, 'I also know the extent of your ill-gotten wealth, and I demand answers. How did you amass such riches? Have you traded your integrity for the royal family's favor? You are a shameless puppet, exploiting your wealth in disgraceful ways.'

As Chinnappa came closer, he said angrily, 'Your father didn't help me at all. My success is because of hard work and support from the villagers. I became who I am through my effort. Now, leave my property, or I'll get the police involved.'

Aditya wasn't scared. He looked right back at Chinnappa and said with anger, 'You can make all the threats you want, but I won't stop until I find out what happened to my father. I'll get to the truth, no matter what.'

Aditya's mother arrived and pulled him away from the confrontation. The tension between Aditya and Chinnappa remained, waiting to explode someday.

But then, a month later, Chinnappa died in a mysterious accident.

The demise of Chinnappa cast suspicions upon Aditya. He found himself in a pivotal phase of his life. Concerned for his future, both his mother and grandmother expressed their worry. This concern served as a catalyst for Aditya to shift his focus towards self-improvement and the pursuit of a stable, fulfilling life. At that time, Aditya was sixteen years old and, while he had found recognition as a district-level kabaddi player, he lacked a clear sense of direction regarding his future. There were no specific skills, career aspirations, or educational pursuits guiding his path.

As the years went by, Aditya embarked on a journey of self-discovery. He began to acknowledge and appreciate his strengths and understand his limitations, all while taking stock of the resources at his disposal, which included a four-acre agricultural plot and a family home. Before he could contemplate any form of revenge against those who had wronged his family, he recognized the importance of first establishing himself in a stable, self-reliant position.

Aditya's situation was unique. Though the sole son of his family, his education had not been a focus of substantial investment as he lacked interest in studies and suffered from mild dyslexia, could be because of the disappointment after his father's death. However, his mother had diligently saved a modest sum from their agricultural activities over the years. With this financial foundation and his exposure to diverse places through kabaddi tournaments, Aditya identified an unexplored opportunity in the market—the sanitary ware business in the town nearby. In the year 2002, he decided to take the plunge into this industry, determined to create a secure future for himself. His mother and his grandmother helped him with the savings they accumulated and hence it wasn't that difficult for Aditya to start the business.

Over time, his business venture proved to be successful, and in 2005, he took another significant step by marrying Vandana. Life appeared to be moving in a positive direction, yet there was a lingering void that troubled Aditya deeply—the unsolved mystery of his father's demise. At that juncture of his life, Aditya stumbled upon the treasure, setting the stage for the next chapter in his life.

On that day, 06th June 2008, Aditya's young mind was only filled with thoughts of the treasure, although he understood that the treasure, in itself, wasn't his ultimate goal but merely a means to achieve it. Yet, there was a lingering unease about the thought of encountering a snake in wake and in sleep.

Sometimes, the things we strongly try to forget can unintentionally seep into the deepest corners of our subconscious. The act of attempting to banish a thought often oddly reinforces it, making it all the more persistent. It's as if the more we resist, the stronger the thought becomes, ultimately imprinting itself into our memory. True forgetting, on the other hand, is a natural process that occurs over time without conscious effort.

He was sure, he would encounter the snake in his dream, as Naagam's wife narrated and as the legends circulated. He looked at the roof, it was not a tiles roof, not a wooden plank one, it was a perfect plane concrete one. He was determined to face the snake in his dream and went into sleep but not a deeper one at least in the first hours. Whenever he was conscious of his sleep, he was reminded of the snake that came face to face. Only after hours Aditya drifted into a deep sleep, the expected moment started to happen.

With its smoothly curved triangular face, the snake loomed just a few centimeters away, right in front of his closed eyes. As it drew nearer, intricate patterns on its shining skin became noticeable, each perfect scale coming into focus, creating a fascinating pattern.

Fangs extended and hanging just below its nostril-like openings, the snake nearly grazed Aditya's forehead, its mouth firmly shut. The fangs seemed to move across his face, and started to lick his cheeks while its muscular body coiled around his chest.

Aditya, lost in his dream, acted unconsciously. He struggled to move his hand, attempting to seize the snake's head, but they remained still. He called out for his mother, seeking rescue, all the while attempting to push the mystic serpent away. His efforts proved unsuccessful; his hands and voice wouldn't respond. Only his closed eyes moved around unpredictably, like a bouncing ball in an enclosed space.

Moments later, his thoughts wavered between dream and reality. One part of him believed it was just a dream, while another part strongly disagreed, urging him to act immediately. After a prolonged internal struggle, the belief that it was merely a dream finally dawned on him. In such situations, he realized, the best course of action was to wake up and he did.

A slight sheen of sweat covered his body, a proof to the intensity of the dream he had just experienced. He could feel his heart racing as he glanced around the room, finding it empty and quiet. The clock on the wall indicated that there were still several hours left until dawn.

Thoughts of his pregnant wife filled his mind, intensifying his sense of responsibility for both their lives. He now felt a greater need to ensure his safety, knowing that he was not only accountable for his own well-being but also for a new life. His fears seemed to magnify in the stillness of the night.

Feeling thirsty and needing to cool down after the intense dream, Aditya quietly got up from his bed. He moved slowly and carefully to avoid disturbing his mother in the nearby room. He needed no efforts to switch on the lights, the moonlight streaming in through the windows illuminated the room. He picked up a glass from the shelf, filled it with water from a clay container and took a small, soothing sip, the refreshing feeling helping to calm the fear he felt from his strange dream.

He withstood the dream in its harshest form. Determined to shake it off, he turned on the TV and drifted into slumber. This time, there were no snakes, not even a pesky insect invading his dreams. It turned out to be one of the most peaceful sleeps he had experienced.

The next morning, amidst the morning bustle of the kitchen, Aditya's mother was busy chopping potatoes and tomatoes, the rhythmic thud of her knife filling the air with a comforting sound. Aditya, seated on the wooden threshold, was enjoying a cup of tea, also recollecting the dreadful dream. Suddenly, Aditya's friend Rakesh entered the house, greeted by the inviting scent of tea and the promise of a hearty meal. His cheerful presence added a lively dimension to the scene, and he joined Aditya sitting on the veranda beside the wooden threshold. Aditya's mother, in the midst of her culinary duties, couldn't help but notice his arrival.

As his mother meticulously prepared food, she glanced over at Aditya. 'Why did you watch TV for so long? I heard it,' she inquired, extending a steaming cup of tea toward him and Rakesh.

Aditya accepted the tea, his brows furrowing as he replied, 'No, Mom, my legs pained so much that I couldn't sleep. It was a hectic day yesterday; I plowed the land for long hours.'

His friend Rakesh, couldn't help but interject with a chuckle, 'Oh, Aditya, did you plow the land alone, or did the bulls too joined you?'

Aditya shot Rakesh a glare before responding, 'I think you don't take bulls to plough, right.'

Concern softened his mother's expression. 'The end-summer heat is deceiving; don't strain yourself or the bulls too much,' she advised. 'By the way, is there enough water in the tank for the bulls from yesterday?'

Aditya paused, realizing he hadn't attended to the bulls the last evening. He inquired, 'Why, any problem?'

She continued her chopping, explaining, 'They didn't graze since yesterday, so I made them stand near the water in the backyard this morning. They consumed a lot.'

'Oh, I see. I'll take care of it,' Aditya assured her, mentally noting to attend to the bulls after breakfast.

Between sips of tea, he broached a different topic. 'Mom, I'm planning to plant mango trees this year itself on our land.'

His mother, her attention still focused on her culinary task, gently reminded him, 'Your plan was for next year, I thought.'

Aditya nodded, adding, 'Yes, Mom, but it would be difficult for me to travel frequently as I have to take care of Nishitha.'

Concerned about the financial aspect, she cautioned, 'But what about the investment? Planting mango trees on four acres is costly.'

'I can manage, Mom. It shouldn't be a problem,' Aditya reassured her, with a determined flash in his eyes.

Out of context, Aditya raised a matter of deep concern in the presence of his close friend, Rakesh, and his ever-supportive mother.

'Ma, now that Rakesh is here, I need to tell you both that I've decided to file a PIL regarding Father's disappearance,' Aditya declared, his tone marked by a mix of anger and maturity etched on his face.

His mother, ever the voice of caution, responded, 'You've been talking about this for years, Adhi. Please don't waste your time. Don't let your future be tainted like your father's.'

Puzzled, Rakesh intervened, 'I've heard you mention this PIL before, but I must admit, I still don't quite grasp it.'

Concerned about the potential expenses, Aditya's mother inquired, 'Isn't it costly to file such a petition?'

Rakesh, genuinely curious, interjected, 'But isn't a PIL typically filed for public interest rather than personal reasons?'

Aditya, his conviction unwavering, explained, 'In this case, a PIL is entirely justified because there's a clear conspiracy surrounding the father's disappearance. He, along with his friend, went missing, and rumors have circulated that they absconded with the treasure. Adding to the mystery, the police have not registered a case.'

Eager to understand, Rakesh probed further, 'Could you elaborate on the conspiracy theory?'

Aditya's reply left them astounded. 'I strongly suspect Prakash Devan's involvement in all of this,' he asserted. 'On the day Father vanished, he, along with Vikram uncle, had visited Prakash Devan continuously for many days. They held secret meetings and then Father returned to the village. Later, when we confirmed Father's disappearance, Prakash Devan simply pretended to be diligently searching for the missing man. He never pressured us to file a complaint with the police. Given his education and awareness, why didn't he take the initiative to file a PIL?'

With curiosity, Rakesh asked, 'But what leads you to believe that Prakash Devan is involved?'

Aditya confidently explained, 'I believe there's a larger conspiracy at play here. If you've noticed, ever since Father and Vikram's uncle disappeared, the focus shifted solely to the missing individuals. All discussions, trials, and movements to preserve Shivan's pride moment declined.'

Rakesh, still grappling with the idea, inquired, 'How can one substantiate such a conspiracy?'

Aditya continued, his voice laced with conviction, 'Do you see anyone talking about Shivan's pride moment now? Look at the fake stories of King Yasho Mardhana circulating across the state. The government turns a deaf ear when asked to declare the sacrifice officially. Don't you see there is a larger conspiracy run by the royal family?'

'But isn't the process of PIL long, hectic, and demanding of money?' queried his mother.

'It certainly is,' replied Aditya.

'But before we proceed, let's delve into the process of PIL,' suggested Rakesh.

'Absolutely, and in the meantime, let's maintain complete confidentiality regarding this PIL plan,' said Aditya.

Aditya took a few days to chalk out the final plan – from excavation of the treasure to liquidizing it. The planning was simple - cultivating maize would give an opportunity to carry out the digging process of the treasure easily and on a rainy night when the maize was grown, he would dig out the treasure and carry it in his Maruti van to store it in the house securely. But to execute it, he had to establish a lot before.

And the cultivation plan dynamically changed from cotton to mango orchid to maize.

Once he finalized the plan, he approached his Mother, 'Maa, how about we cultivate maize this time? No more mangoes, no cotton, and no chilies, please,' Aditya proposed, concealing his true intention to his mother who was bundling the hay to store it for the rest of the year for the bulls.

Aditya knew that maize plants grew rapidly, and their height could reach six feet in just three months, which would make it easier for him to carry out his secret plan of digging for the treasure chest.

His mother looked puzzled, 'But last year, the cotton crop brought in a good profit, and everyone in the village seems to be leaning towards it this year too,' she replied, putting aside a bundle on the heap.

Aditya sighed, knowing he had to persuade her. 'This year, we won't have much time to dedicate to cultivation. Vandana needs more care, and I'll be traveling more frequently to town and to Vandana's village.'

His mother nodded thoughtfully. 'Up to you, Aadhi. Just a few days ago, you were keen on starting a mango orchard, and now its maize.'

Aditya gathered the loose hay and started to fold it to make a bundle in support to his mother and spoke with determination, 'Listen to me this year, Maa. I have my plans, trust me.'

She sighed, realizing that Aditya had made up his mind. 'All right, but the only problem will be safeguarding it from the wild pigs and birds,' she cautioned.

Aditya reassured her, 'Leave it to me, Maa. I'll take care of everything.'

The next day, Aditya made a significant shift in his daily routine. He dedicated the morning hours, before lunch, to his agricultural work. Post-lunch, his focus shifted to the shop, which was usually managed by a dedicated full-time employee. Aditya started to return home late, typically around 9 or 10 at night.

Before seeding the maize, he made the most to nourish the soil with a rich blend of nutrients. Aditya ensured the soil received ample organic manure and vermicomposting, and he tirelessly tilled the land repeatedly to ensure the compost is evenly distributed across the land. His aim was simple: he wanted the maize crop to reach its maximum height, soon.

Aditya was meticulous in every aspect of his farming. He carefully selected the best seeds and pesticides, never compromising on quality. He was determined to eliminate any potential risks that could jeopardize his crop.

Aditya made a notable change in his commute between the village and the shop in the town. He switched from using his bike to using his Maruti van, which provided him with more convenience, especially given his increasingly busy schedule.

Once a week, he set aside time to visit his in-laws' house, where he cherished moments with Vandana, his wife. This newfound dedication to his work and family earned him the affectionate nickname 'busy bee' from those around him, a title he was determined to be spread in the circles.

Aditya also ensured that his routine and schedule was known to everyone around him – first half of the day was for agriculture, the second half till 9 PM was for the sanitary ware shop and every Sunday to his in-law's house for Vandana.

Lessons learnt from Naagam's story Aditya ensured all the tools to dig the treasure site were available in multiple set among the maize crop.

As the weeks passed, Aditya's anticipation grew, waiting for the opportune moment to unearth the treasure concealed beneath his thriving maize field. With meticulous care, he observed the maize crop's progress, patiently awaiting the day it would exceed the desired height of five feet.

The maize crop progressed and for him to continue his plan he yearned for a specific type of rain after 8 PM – one that would pour down so heavily that it would frighten people from venturing outside, a downpour so dense that it would extinguish the lights. Every day, he kept a watchful eye on the sky from the balcony of his shop, hoping for the right kind of rain. In this forested region, nestled near the hills, such torrential rains were almost guaranteed during that season – between September and October.

Months passed for Aditya without missing the routine. Then, in the mid of September, the moment he had been waiting for arrived. The rain had been falling relentlessly since morning, punctuated by only brief pauses that lasted for not more than few minutes. The clouds looked promising to continue to rain for more than a day. It was an undeclared holiday in many districts due to the weather. People in the village of Jhagaram completed the important tasks before noon and decided to have fun for two more days as they were sure of the continued downpour. Added to the situation, the farmers too had not much work as the crops crossed the early stage and required at least a month to harvest some of them like Maize and Paddy.

He was confident that the rain would persist for at least two more days; this forecast had also been substantiated by weather reports in the media. The government had issued alerts, urging the public to avoid traveling to waterlogged areas and advising them to stay home, as roads were inundated by floods. The downpour had caused power outages due to damage to electrical transformers. But then, Aditya deliberately set off for his shop after lunch, disregarding his mother's warnings.

As Aditya arrived at his shop in the town, he noticed his employee preparing to close up for the day, assuming that his boss wouldn't come due to the heavy rain.

'Hey, calling it a day?' Aditya inquired, addressing the employee who was pulling down the shop's shutter.

'Yes, boss. No customers today, and I don't expect anyone to come today or tomorrow,' the employee replied, starting to lift the shutter back.

'True, the rain is quite heavy,' Aditya agreed as he entered the shop.

'Yes, sir. It is supposed to continue for two more days,' the employee added.

'Have you had lunch at least?' Aditya asked, taking a seat.

'No, sir. Not yet. I was planning to head home,' the employee replied.

'Anyway, since we might not have any customers today and tomorrow, here's what you can do. Take the phone numbers of our debtors from the accounts register and follow up with them to payback. If the rain lets up, visit their houses,' Aditya instructed.

'Sure, sir. I'll take care of it. You should also take a break, sir. Lately, you've been working too hard,' the employee remarked subtly.

'Absolutely, I plan to wrap up the accounts today and take a short vacation to visit my in-laws home' Aditya shared.

'Sir, that's a good idea. You should spend quality time with Madam during this break,' the employee advised.

If there was anyone who wished for the rain to continue and intensify, it was the school children and, perhaps, Aditya. After the employee had left for the day, Aditya found himself peering out of the window. The downpour showed no signs of letting up; in fact, it seemed to be increasing in intensity. Beyond a meter or so from the window, everything was shrouded in a curtain of rain. The road that ran in front of the shop had turned into a flowing stream.

Aditya patiently waited for more than six hours before finally deciding to close the shop. His was the only establishment open in that weather; even the emergency vehicle repair shops had pulled their shutters down. During those hours of waiting, Aditya meticulously rehearsed his plan and double-checked every tool he intended to carry with him.

At seven O'clock, Aditya started to the treasure site with his essentials packed in a carry bag: his trusty leather beetle shoes, rubber gloves, and a headlight. As he navigated the tough road in his Maruthi van, the rain poured relentlessly, reducing visibility to a mere guess. Aditya's years of experience on this challenging route served as his guide. For anyone else, this wouldn't even qualify as a road. Both the van's wipers and Aditya's heartbeat raced at their highest speeds, but he knew he had to remain composed. Apart from one or two heavy vehicles, the journey was weirdly quiet.

What should have been a twenty-minute trip took Aditya an hour due to the heavy rain that reduced visibility. Upon reaching the treasure site, he parked the van so close to the crop that some maize plants half-covered it. Aditya disembarked, clad in his beetle shoes, rubber gloves, and raincoat, with the trusty headlight illuminating his way. The tools were already lying in the farm for a month. It was not difficult for him to find them and reach to the treasure spot. Kneeling beside the maize plants, he carefully located the spot where he had buried the iron ring a few months ago.

Aditya's first step was to use a shovel to locate the iron ring buried in the soil. Once he found it, he grabbed the chain attached to the iron ring, followed it for a few feats where it got tightened and did not move, signaling the treasure spot. With his rubber-gloved hands securely gripping the digging bar, Aditya braced himself against the relentless rain. Aditya firmly gripped the digging bar, and the rubber glove helped him maintain a secure hold, even as the rain kept soaking the bar.

The black soil, known for its sticky nature, clung to the bar as Aditya began to dig. However, Aditya had prepared for this challenge by carrying two digging bars and a handful of small shovels. With skillful precision, he scraped off the mud clinging to the bar every two to three strikes. Despite the meticulous pace of progress, Aditya remained resolute in his mission. The rain, merciless, continued to pour down like a barrage of bullets upon his drenched figure. He continued while his heart pounded with a mixture of excitement and nervousness. With each scoop he did, the soil became heavy and clung to the shovel and the digging rod. Aditya's hands trembled as he dug deeper, his anticipation growing with every passing moment. He knew he was getting closer to the hidden treasure.

Finally, after what felt like an eternity, the bar hit something hard. Aditya's heart raced as he brushed away the sticky soil to reveal an old, weathered jar under four feet deep. He dug around the exposed part of the jar and kept on clearing and then, there it was – the opening of the jar, tightly sealed with a cap and screws.

His breath caught as he examined the jar more closely. The cap is fixed securely to the body with screws. Determined

Aditya reached for the hammer and with a calculated precision, he worked to loosen the screws that held the cap in place.

The cap had four screws and Aditya smashed one after the other. As the final screw gave way, his heart raced. He carefully removed the cap, his hands trembling with a mixture of apprehension and awe. And then, his eyes fell upon it – a sight that left him momentarily breathless. Gold, gleaming and precious, lay nestled within the jar, a treasure trove of unbearable weight physically and mentally.

His hands trembled as he reached into the jar, carefully lifting a piece of gold, letting its weight and significance sink in. As he knelt there, Aditya's heart raced as he delicately plucked a single gold coin from the sea of hundreds that lay within the jar along with thick chains and lockets. The coin shined in his hand, its radiant surface reflecting the dim light of his headlamp. He marveled at its beauty, at its history yet he simultaneously oscillated between the dream and reality. The weight of the gold in his hand was not just a physical sense; it was a symbol of hope, possibility and power to him to uncover the truth about his father's mysterious disappearance. The gold coin he held was not just a piece of metal; it was a symbol of his unwavering resolve to seek justice and unearth the truth. It was a symbol of his determination to honor his father's memory and prove his innocence, no matter the challenges that lay ahead.

Aditya became unconscious to the cold, harsh reality of the thunder-struck rainy night. Instead, he was lost in the moment, in the significance of what he had found. The raindrops that soaked him were mere tickling against the backdrop of his newfound power.

In that instant, Aditya felt a surge of strength and purpose coursing through him.

With a sudden jolt of realization, Aditya understood the urgency of the situation. He knew he had to leave the site promptly to avoid any suspicion or concern arising from his prolonged absence.

Swiftly, he retrieved a leather bag from his backpack and commenced the delicate task of transferring the precious gold. Each coin, chain, bracelets and lockets were handled with the utmost care, ensuring that not a single one slipped through his trembling fingers. As the bag filled, the weight in his hands grew substantially.

Aditya estimated that the leather bag now held around forty kilograms of the gleaming treasure. Yet, when he glanced back at the jar, it was evident that it still harbored an equal amount of gold. Time was of the essence, and he knew he had to make his exit swiftly.

With a sense of urgency and excitement coursing through his veins, Aditya concealed the iron ring and its chain within the pit. Now the iron ring and the chain were more than four feet deep in the soil, more safe from apprehensions in mind and the pigs on field. He expertly plucked several maize plants at random and replanted them over the treasure's hiding place, ensuring that the area seamlessly blended in with the rest of the crop. The tools he had used were carefully returned to their usual spots, erasing any trace of his secret endeavor.

As he made his way back to the waiting van, Aditya placed the weighty leather bag, filled with a fortune in gold, onto the back seat. It rested amidst cartons filled with sanitary ware materials.

Once inside the van, he shed his gloves, raincoat, and beetle shoe, cherishing the momentousness of his daring act. With the van's engine revving to life, he embarked on the journey homeward. The pouring rain couldn't dampen his spirits, and he drove with an eager heart.

His arrival at home was punctuated by his mother's presence at the door, waiting anxiously for him due to the unrelenting rain.

Aditya parked the van in its usual spot, ensuring all the windows were securely closed and the lights switched off. As he stepped out of the vehicle, he braced himself for the confrontation he knew was coming.

His mother's voice pierced through the heavy rain as she scolded him for his late arrival. Aditya, avoiding her gaze, calmly responded, 'No, Maa, I'm on time as usual.' He didn't want to show the anxiety that was roiling within him.

His mother's worry was tangible. 'I was just about to call your friends for help. I was so concerned with this heavy rain.'

Aditya reassured her, 'I had been waiting at the shop, hoping the rain would wane, but it looked like it's going to continue all night. I considered staying at the shop, but I knew you'd be worried, hence I came home.'

His mother, in her usual caring manner, had hot water ready on the stove for him. 'The water's still hot; you can use it for your bath.'

'Ok Maa,' Aditya replied gratefully. 'I'm feeling quite hungry as well. Please have some food ready for me; I'll eat right after I'm done with my bath.' With those words, he headed to the bathroom, his heart still racing from the daring endeavor.

The much needed hot water bath helped him calm down mentally and physically. The muscles that strained, the palms that went cramps, got released off from the stress, provided much-needed relief, soothing his strained muscles and calming his nerves. It eased the cramps in his palms, released tension in his shoulders and neck, and cooled his head. He emerged from the bath feeling near to normal.

After a rather unsatisfying supper, Aditya's mother retired to her room and quickly drifted off to sleep. Aditya, however, found himself restless. He started to watch TV, waiting for his time until he was certain his mother was deeply asleep. Once assured of her slumber, he retrieved the bag of gold from the van and made his way to the small prayer room tucked away in a quiet corner of the house.

Guided by the beam of a torch, he examined the contents of the bag he had carefully retrieved from the hidden jar. Spread out before him on the floor was a glittering treasure trove of great gold jewelry. Thick chains, an array of lockets, exquisite bracelets, and dense bangles shimmered in the torchlight. Among these treasures, a substantial number of gold coins bore the emblem of the ancient Vijetha kingdom – a bullock cart.

Aditya realized that he needed to handle this newfound wealth discreetly. He decided to safeguard the treasure at two places. The gold coins, marked with the symbol of the kingdom, found their place in the storeroom among items that had collected dust for years. In the storeroom were large brass vessels, traditionally reserved for gifting to daughters on their wedding day. These vessels now rested on a forgotten shelf, shrouded in spider webs and surrounded by rat droppings, undisturbed for many months. Aditya was well aware that trading the gold coins, which bore the kingdom's symbol, would be challenging.

The other part of the treasure, comprising the glittering chains and lockets, he carefully packed them in a cloth bag and arranged on a shelf in the prayer room behind the baskets that contained rarely used sacred material. The prayer, usually in any house hold, has access to only the family members and in the house of Aditya, the shelf where he placed the gold can only be accessed by him due to its height. Whenever something on the shelf was needed, his mother had to wait for Aditya. Also the prayer room, seldom used for anything beyond daily cleaning, was typically untouched except during major festivals such as Dasara, Diwali, Pongal, and Ugadi. The room itself housed old photographs, sacred idols, and various prayer-related items, and a shelf in it belonged to his grandmother, which was not touched by anyone and hence the prayer room became an infrequently visited space in their home.

After careful placing of the treasure, Aditya felt confident to sleep peacefully. "It's been quite a while since he spoke affectionately to his mother, granny, and friends. "He felt the burden upon him release and when he woke, everything around him seemed profound to him.

He noticed that the brush toothbrush he had been using is not worth it as the bristles sunk.

'Is the tea powder you used today different?' Asked Aditya when his mother served him the regular tea.

'No, the regular one. Why? Is it not good?'

'It is awesome maa.' Said Aditya relishing the sips.

'This is the same tea since years.' Said her mother walking towards the backyard to attend the bulls.

'Hey granny,' Aditya carried another cup of tea and walked to the bed where his granny was sitting. She became so old that she wasn't able to walk, she could only sit or sleep. Her ears and eyes were at their lowest.

'Have this granny.' Aditya or anyone had to talk in a louder voice to reach her ears however she got so used to the gestures and actions to understand the routine communication.

'Where is your mother?' Asked Granny, her voice unclear due to the absence of teeth, however, Aditya understood her voice.

'She went to the backyard Granny, could be to attend the bulls.' Said Aditya, moving closer to her.

'How is the shop working for you?' Enquired Granny.

'I doubled your investment, you want it back, tell me granny.' Said Aditya, the usual response, in a humorous tone to thank her for supporting with investment in the beginning.

'Don't joke, tell me, how is it going now, swear on me.' Reiterated Granny while the tears rolled onto her cheeks.

'I swear, Granny, I swear on you. I am happy with the income, and you know, in just a year, I am opening two more shops, such is the blessing of yours.' Said Aditya and consoled her.

'If there is anything that is making me to die in peace is to see you happy, stay blessed always.' She couldn't control her tears while Aditya held her shoulders and consoled her saying, 'you have lived such a great life Granny, I am proud of you.'

From that day onward, another highly important and urgent task emerged – liquefying the treasure. Aditya's tactics for liquidating the treasure were nothing short of intricate and cunning. Armed with a vast network of friends and acquaintances, he embarked on this complex journey with the utmost care.

To begin with, he utilized his far-reaching connections. Aditya reached out to friends living in various regions, cleverly selecting individuals who were far from each other to prevent any potential communication. He didn't stop there; he also approached his in-laws, knowing that involving his extended family would further diversify his circle of trust.

Aditya's true genius shone through when he employed the strategy of presenting the gold as a family inheritance, supposedly passed down from his grandmother. He capitalized on the deeply ingrained belief that selling gold was not just a financial transaction but also a matter of prestige and family honor. He also reasoned for his act of selling the gold that he was venturing into another business and he needed investment. This narrative not only served as a cover story but also ensured that those involved would be motivated to maintain secrecy, as the reputation of Aditya's family was seemingly at stake.

Through skillful persuasion, he approached very few but he convinced each person to treat the matter with the utmost discretion. This helped him sell it without anyone getting too curious or suspicious. As part of his ingenious plan, Aditya devised another strategy to liquidate the gold. He cleverly sought out private lenders who specialized in offering loans with gold as collateral. Initially, he utilized the treasure as security to secure loans. However, over time, he simulated financial difficulties, artfully fabricating an inability to repay the loans.

This calculated move allowed Aditya to give the impression that he was in dire financial stress, and in adherence to the loan agreements, the lenders gradually took possession of the gold.

The element of risk in this approach was undeniable, but it enabled Aditya to systematically distribute the gold to different parties. By doing so, he made it exceptionally challenging for anyone to trace the origin of the treasure and comfortably liquidate without harming anyone. Additionally, Aditya's smart choice of private lenders spread across diverse locations added an extra layer of complexity to the situation. The geographical dispersion of these lenders further obstructed the flow of information and gossip, rendering it virtually impossible for any rumors to circulate widely. The beauty of Aditya's strategy lay not only in its intricate execution but also in its calculated subtlety, ensuring that his pursuit of justice remained a closely guarded secret.

Aditya spent a year more in converting all the gold into other assets by investing in agricultural land, real estate, and new gold.

The Revenge Plan

Aditya sat nervously in the lawyer's office, his fingers tapping lightly on his knee as he began to recount the events of the past and rehearsing the phrases to communicate to the lawyer. Aditya had interacted with that lawyer twice a few days back to seek his appointment by briefing his thoughts. The lawyer, a middle-aged man known for his professionalism, finally gave him an appointment on a Sunday as Aditya persisted for a long discussion and said that money was not at all an issue.

An hour later, the lawyer walked into the office with his assistant.

The lawyer, perched forward in his chair, set the stage for their conversation. 'Mr. Aditya, let's start from the beginning. Tell me about your father, Raghava, and his friend Vikram. What were they like?'

Aditya, momentarily lost in thought, carefully composed his response. 'Well, my father, Raghava, was a determined and principled man. He believed in justice and was deeply committed to the cause of recognizing the sacrifice of the twenty-one soldiers in the Shivan's Pride moment. He, along with Vikram, played a crucial role in organizing events and advocating for their recognition.'

The lawyer, acknowledging the introduction with a nod, directed the conversation to the events preceding their disappearance, 'I see. And what can you tell me about the events leading up to their disappearance?'

Aditya, sighing as he delved into the turbulent past, recounted, 'It was a turbulent time. The Shivan's Pride moment was gaining momentum, and the demand for official recognition was growing louder. My father and Vikram were at the forefront of it all. But then, one day, they went missing.'

Raising an eyebrow, the lawyer sought clarification, 'Missing, you say? Were there any leads or investigations at the time?'

Aditya, frowning at the haunting memories, revealed, 'That's the thing, there wasn't much of an investigation. My mother reported their disappearance to the police, but they didn't seem to take it seriously. No case was filed, and no efforts were made to find them. It was as if their voices had been silenced.'

Furrowing his brow, the lawyer pressed further, 'that's concerning. Why do you think the police were reluctant to investigate?'

Aditya, hesitating, shared unsettling rumors, 'It's hard to say for sure, but there were rumors - unsettling rumors. Some said that my father and Vikram had stumbled upon something, something big, related to the treasure hidden in our forests. And there were whispers of foul play involving powerful individuals.'

Leaning back, the lawyer absorbed this information, 'I see. So, you believe their disappearance might be connected to this treasure?'

Aditya, nodding with conviction, asserted, 'Yes, that's one of the possibilities. But what baffles me is that even those in key positions within the Shivan's Pride moment didn't push for an investigation. It was as if everyone went silent, afraid of something or someone.'

Steeling his fingers, the lawyer acknowledged the gravity of the situation, 'I understand your concerns, Mr. Aditya. However, filing a Public Interest Litigation (PIL) after such a long time can be challenging. Unless we have new and compelling evidence, it might be difficult to pursue.'

Resolute, Aditya expressed his determination, 'I know it won't be easy, but I can't let this go. If there's any chance to uncover the truth, to bring justice to my father and Vikram, I'll take it. We need answers, not just for our family but for all those who believed in Shivan's pride moment.'

Nodding in acknowledgment, the lawyer commended Aditya's determination, 'I admire your determination, Mr. Aditya. Let's explore our options further. We'll need to gather as much information as possible and see if there are any legal avenues we can pursue.'

Expressing gratitude, Aditya replied, 'Thank you, sir. I'll do whatever it takes to find out the truth and honor my father's legacy.'

The lawyer and Aditya continued their conversation, delving deeper into the details and potential avenues for their quest for justice.

The lawyer, leaning forward with a seriousness that underscored the gravity of the situation, directed the conversation. 'Mr. Aditya, do you have any suspicions about who might be behind your father and Vikram's disappearance?'

Aditya, in a moment of contemplation, responded, 'Well, it's hard to say for sure, but there is one person who raises a lot of questions - Prakash Devan. My father and Vikram used to meet him occasionally, but during the week they went missing, they met almost every day. And the strange thing is, when we confronted Prakash Devan about it, he denied meeting them. I was just an eight-year-old kid at that time, but I distinctly remember how they would talk about Prakash Devan every evening after the meeting.'

The lawyer, raising an eyebrow in anticipation, inquired further, 'That does sound suspicious. Why do you think Prakash Devan might be involved?'

Aditya, choosing his words carefully, expressed his thoughts, 'It's hard to put my finger on it, but it's the timing that bothers me the most. The sudden increase in meetings right before their disappearance, Prakash Devan's denial, and the fact that he was somewhat connected to the Shivan's pride moment – it all seems too coincidental.'

Nodding in acknowledgment, the lawyer affirmed, 'I understand your concerns, Mr. Aditya. We'll certainly need to look into this further. It might be a crucial piece of the puzzle.'

Their conversation unfolded as they discussed the potential involvement of Prakash Devan, recognizing the need for a thorough investigation into this perplexing case.

The lawyer, furrowing his brow, delved into another aspect, 'Mr. Aditya, it's puzzling that no case was filed, and no one seemed to pressurize the authorities to take action. Can you shed some light on why that might be?'

Aditya, sighing as he revisited a painful chapter in their history, shared, 'It's a painful part of our family's history. At that time, I was just a kid, and my mother, well, she was overwhelmed and not familiar with legal processes. She was lost in her own grief and responsibilities. Vikram uncle, he was unmarried and living with his elderly parents. I guess everyone was dealing with their struggles, and no one came forward to fight for my father and Vikram uncle.'

Expressing sympathy, the lawyer acknowledged the complexity of the situation, 'I see. It's undoubtedly a complex situation. We'll need to consider all these factors as we move forward.'

Their conversation continued, with the lawyer gaining a deeper understanding of the family's circumstances and the challenges they faced during those difficult times.

Contemplating the path ahead, the lawyer sought Aditya's perspective, 'So, Mr. Aditya, what would you like our objective to be in this matter?'

Aditya, firm in his resolve, asserted, 'Our primary objective should be to initiate an investigation. I strongly believe that Prakash Devan had some connections with the royal family, and this disappearance is not as simple as it seems. I want the truth to come out, and if there's any wrongdoing involved, justice must be served. Let there be a thorough investigation into my father's and Vikram's disappearance.'

Nodding in agreement, the lawyer affirmed, 'Understood, Mr. Aditya. We'll work towards uncovering the truth and seeking justice through the appropriate legal channels.'

Aditya had a clear strategy in mind: to involve both the legal system and the public in Shivan's moment. He knew that for any substantial change to happen, the issue needed to be recognized as significant both by the judiciary and the masses, only then the Government could focus on it. So, he embarked on a dual-track approach.

First, he filed a Public Interest Litigation (PIL), a legal move made more accessible with the help of the skilled lawyer. This was the path to engage the judiciary, where he aimed to have the sacrifices of the twenty-one soldiers officially recognized and to uncover the conspiracy surrounding his father's death.

The second path was a bit trickier: engaging the public. Aditya understood that Shivan's moment needed to be a movement owned by the people. To achieve this, he reactivated the Shivan's pride movement to spread the word and rally public support through protests and awareness campaigns.

As soon as the PIL was filed, action on the ground began. Donation camps sprang up across the state, manned and funded by Aditya. Aditya's intention was mainly to create a sensation to gather the attention of the state and the tool he had was a lot of money.

The story of the sacrifice of soldiers was printed in many formats – from one-page story to a booklet and was randomly distributed at crowded areas like colleges, malls, and sports grounds. Along with the distribution of promotional material, fund mobilization campaigns were organized simultaneously. Some young and motivated were employed as volunteers for fifteen days who were paid a nominal amount to reach out to ordinary individuals and small business owners, urging them to contribute to Shivan's moment. Donation boxes found their place in local shops, where people could give what they could. The demands were clear: to recognize the truth about the soldiers' sacrifice and to honor their bravery.

In that state-wide campaign, volunteers took to the streets. Each volunteer carried a locked collection box, ensuring the security of the funds collected.

At the end of each day, the collection boxes were opened only by Aditya. Aditya knew that the public donations would be very little but Aditya added his money every day to the account and ensured to total that sum to one crore rupees – It is through a huge sum, he wanted to create a talk, a sensation, and garner the attention of the media. As planned, he released a note to the press and advertised in all the prominent new papers.

His press release captured the attention of various media houses, and he was approached for interviews by numerous outlets. However, Aditya opted for the most prominent one. In the bustling TV studio, Aditya made his entrance, dressed in a full shirt with the sleeves neatly folded, a pair of jeans, and comfortable sports shoes. The live TV show had invited him for an interview following his press release that the Shivan's Pride movement had garnered a staggering donation of over one crore rupees.

The journalist wasted no time in getting to the heart of the matter. 'One crore rupees in just a month?' he asked with a mix of curiosity and awe, clearly impressed by the enormity of the amount.

Aditya responded confidently, 'Yes, one crore, three lakhs, fifty-six thousand, and eight hundred rupees, to be exact. And all of it is safely deposited in the bank.'

The journalist couldn't hide his intrigue. 'Is the collection still ongoing?' he inquired.

Aditya shook his head. 'No, we decided to halt it after just a month.'

The journalist probed further, 'was it your intention to stop, or was it a part of your plan?'

Aditya explained, 'Our plan was to keep the doors open for donations as long as it took to achieve our objective. However, the response we received was overwhelming, and we felt we had gathered enough funds for now.'

Concerned about handling such a large sum without knowing the donors' identities, the journalist questioned, 'Do you think you can manage such a substantial amount? Aren't you worried about the challenges of handling such huge, anonymous donations?'

Aditya responded thoughtfully, 'The amount is undeniably significant. To put it into perspective, one acre of land in my village costs one lakh rupees. So, the amount we accumulated is equivalent to the value of a hundred acres. We understand the magnitude. What's important to note is that this was achieved through campaigns spanning over fifteen districts.'

The journalist chuckled and shared, 'I recently purchased an acre of land in my village for one lakh rupees.'

Observing the unprecedented nature of the donations, the journalist remarked, 'Nowhere in history has any fund collection campaign received such massive support from the general public in such a short time and that too for a cause which was not known to the public in general.'

Aditya clarified, 'Our primary goal wasn't merely to collect funds. Throughout the process, we disseminated the story of the 'Shivan's Pride' movement. We shared the soldiers' valor through short stories, ranging from single-page narratives to booklets with accompanying pictures. We informed the public about our cause and implored them to support our demand for the government to honor the sacrifices made. Another, you need to correct your statement, that the cause is not known to the public. It is known and it is shown now.'

Aditya cleverly linked and established the context with both the public and the media.

The journalist then inquired about their specific demands, to which Aditya replied, 'We demand that the government overturn the declaration made by the forest department, which dismissed the soldiers' sacrifices as a myth, a verdict later sanctioned by the government itself. We want this decision revoked, and we call upon the government to officially initiate the search for the hidden treasure. Additionally, we urge them to launch a comprehensive investigation into the disappearance of my father and his friend.'

Skeptical about proving an incident that occurred six decades ago, the journalist questioned, 'But how can anyone substantiate an event that transpired sixty years ago?'

Aditya's frustration showed as he responded, 'The sons, daughters, friends, neighbors, and cousins who witnessed the soldiers succumb to poisoning are still alive. We can interview them, get their firsthand accounts.'

Skeptical, the journalist questioned further, 'But how do we know if their accounts are accurate?'

Aditya's anger flared as he retorted, 'Are you suggesting that you don't believe the voices of a hundred witnesses?'

Quickly backtracking, the journalist clarified, 'No, that's not what I meant. What other evidence do you have to prove that the story is true?'

Aditya replied with determination, 'I can prove that someone is influencing the government against us.'

'Who could be that someone? Are you hinting at the royal family?' Asked the journalist.

'I don't want to communicate my speculations now, but a thorough investigation would surely prove it. I can of course give my points to the investigating agency.'

The journalist, questioning the impact of their voter population, commented, 'The government should listen to you first. Why doesn't it listen to you people?'

Aditya explained, 'Our population is concentrated in just one constituency, and that might be the reason. But now, we've garnered support from eighty percent of the constituencies. People have come forward to stand by us, and we're thankful to every individual in the state who has supported our cause.'

Following the callers' expressions of support for the movement, the interviewers wrapped up the program. Aditya expressed his gratitude to the journalist and the entire team before exiting the studio. However, as he reached the reception area, he was taken aback to find Prakash Devan waiting there.

Prakash Devan, a man of distinct presence, made his entrance into the bustling TV studio with an air of unwavering determination. Despite being 58 years old, he appeared remarkably youthful and vigorous. His fair complexion, clean-shaven face, and white hair created a distinguished contrast, and at six feet tall with a well-built physique, he seemed larger than life.

His attire was simple but perfect – a light-colored half-shirt paired with dark trousers, reflecting a no-nonsense approach to dressing. What truly stood out about Prakash Devan, beyond his appearance, was the aura of serenity and self-assurance that enveloped him. He displayed an unspoken wisdom, a quiet confidence that demanded respect from anyone in his presence.

Aditya initially tried to ignore Prakash Devan and continued toward the exit, but Prakash Devan's insistence couldn't be ignored. 'Aditya, come here,' he called out loudly, prompting Aditya to halt in his tracks.

'We were truly great friends, your father, Vikram, and me; we made an exceptional team,' Prakash Devan reminisced.

Aditya replied, avoiding eye contact, 'I'm well aware of that, sir.'

Prakash Devan continued, 'I had wanted to visit you when you were arrested, but I could not. Nonetheless, as they say, God works in mysterious ways, and Chinnappa met a tragic end.'

Aditya nodded solemnly, 'Yes, but it wasn't my wish for Chinnappa.'

Prakash Devan inquired about the interview, 'Are you done with the interview?'

Aditya, taken aback by Prakash Devan's knowledge, replied cautiously, 'Yes, just now. But it wasn't live. How did you know?'

Prakash Devan asserted confidently, 'I have my ways of finding out, my friend. Now it's my turn to share my thoughts on the movement.'

Aditya, his guard up, thanked Prakash Devan and subtly stepped backward, signaling his disinterest in further conversation.

Prakash Devan, however, offered his support, saying, 'I'm always here if you need any assistance with the movement. All the best.'

With that, Prakash Devan walked away toward the studio room, leaving Aditya to deal with his uncertainty about whom to trust in the complex web of the 'Shivan's Pride' movement.

Aditya couldn't escape the feeling of unease when Prakash Devan made his unexpected comeback. The timing was too exact to disregard as a coincidence; Prakash Devan's return matched perfectly with the revival of the 'Shivan's Pride' movement. This raised a persistent suspicion in Aditya's mind - did Prakash Devan possess important information about the past, a secret plan that had once brought their movement crashing down?

For nearly two decades, Prakash Devan had been a mysterious figure staying hidden. And now, just as 'Shivan's Pride' gained momentum once more, he emerged from the shadows. It was a strange repetition of history, resembling the circumstances that had led to the movement's sudden downfall years ago, shortly after Prakash Devan's initial involvement.

Aditya couldn't dismiss the peculiar timing of Prakash Devan's return. It felt as though Prakash Devan had reentered their lives to influence the destiny of the movement once again. This time around, Aditya knew he had to proceed cautiously, unraveling Prakash Devan's intentions, and safeguarding the cherished cause from any potential dangers.

In the studio room, the journalist, seated across from him, observed this seasoned campaigner's arrival. 'Welcome, Mr. Prakash Devan,' she greeted him as he settled into the studio's comfortable chair.

'Thank you,' Prakash Devan replied, his voice carrying the weight of a man who had seen much in his 58 years.

As the interview began, the journalist couldn't help but raise the question that had been on many minds. 'Mr. Prakash Devan, your absence from the public eye for so many years has raised eyebrows. Can you shed light on the reasons behind your return to the forefront of the movement, particularly when Aditya has already taken the reins?'

Prakash Devan leaned forward, his gaze steady. 'Every movement needs a leader, and for a time, we found that leader in Raghava. He was an exceptional man. But we lost him,' he paused, a trace of sadness crossing his eyes. 'Now, his son Aditya has stepped up. He's shown that he's more than capable of leading our cause. I may have been silent, but it's time for me to lend my support to this new generation.'

The journalist pressed further, her curiosity unabated. 'But what prompted your return now, after so many years? What changed?'

Prakash Devan's expression remained unwavering. 'Our movement is like a river, ever-flowing. Sometimes, it needs a familiar hand to guide it through wild routes. The revival of our cause under Aditya's leadership made me realize that my experience and knowledge can be put to good use once again.'

The interview continued, with Prakash Devan shedding light on the challenges they had faced, the unyielding spirit of his community, and the journey that lay ahead.

'Prakash Devan, we've just heard from Aditya about the staggering one crore donation to the 'Shivan's Pride' movement. What's your take on this?' asked the journalist.

'It's undeniably a remarkable achievement. The overwhelming response from the public speaks volumes about the significance of this movement and the people's trust in its objectives,' Prakash Devan extended his wishes to the movement.

'Indeed, it's a considerable sum. Can you share your perspective on what the movement's demands are?' asked the journalist.

'The core demands remain clear. We aim to have the sacrifice of those brave soldiers officially recognized as true. We're also pushing for an official hunt to unearth the hidden treasure and investigate the disappearances of my dear friends Vikram and Raghava. These demands are rooted in justice, honoring those who gave their lives for a noble cause,' he reiterated the stand.

The relentless efforts of the legal team, the extensive coverage of the issue in television debates, and the growing buzz across the state eventually led to a significant development. The high court, acknowledging the mounting evidence and public sentiment, took a decisive step. It ordered a comprehensive investigation into the mysterious disappearance of Vikram and Raghava.

Furthermore, the court urged the government to reconsider its previous stance, wherein it had dismissed the soldiers' sacrifice as a mere myth. It recommended that the government establish an independent commission tasked with the responsibility of delving into the events surrounding Shivan's sacrifice. This commission was expected to delve deep into historical records, testimonies of surviving witnesses, and any available evidence that could shed light on the truth.

The court's actions marked a significant turning point in the 'Shivan's Pride' movement. It not only demonstrated the judiciary's responsiveness to the calls for justice but also indicated a growing recognition of the movement's legitimacy. The commission's impending investigation held the promise of uncovering the long-buried facts about the soldiers' sacrifice and the treasure's whereabouts. It was a momentous step towards the movement's ultimate goal of seeking justice for those who had given their lives for a cause they believed in.

Deputy Inspector General, Ranjith Nayak, a seasoned investigator, on the verge of his retirement, led Aditya into a small, dimly lit room at the police station. The room was functional, with drab gray walls that had borne witness to many investigations but this one was strange. A large rectangular table dominated the center, surrounded by plain wooden chairs. A single window with frosted glass offered a glimpse of the outside world, although it did little to brighten the room.

As Aditya took a seat, he noticed a digital voice recorder placed strategically at the center of the table. Its blinking red light signaled readiness to capture every word of the conversation. On one side of the table sat Inspector Ranjith himself, his badge gleaming under the harsh fluorescent lighting. He was joined by his partner, Ananya, a sharp and attentive officer known for her meticulous note-taking and her comprehension skills along with the desired investigating skills.

The room had an air of formality. Official documents were neatly arranged in a folder, and a sturdy laptop was set up in one corner, ready to document the proceedings. Aditya couldn't help but feel a sense of unease as he waited for the interrogation to begin.

Inspector Ranjith cleared his throat, his demeanor was professional yet slightly intimidating. 'Mr. Aditya,' he began, 'I am DIG Ranjith, and this is Ananya. We're here to discuss the recent developments regarding the 'Shivan's Pride' movement.'

Aditya nodded, a hint of tension in his expression. 'I understand. I'm here to cooperate fully.'

Ananya clicked her pen and poised it over a notepad, ready to record. 'Let's start from the beginning,' she said. 'Tell us about the movement and its objectives.'

Aditya took a deep breath and began recounting the history of the movement, its demands, and the recent surge in public support. He spoke with conviction, knowing the importance of his words in the investigation.

As Aditya spoke, Inspector Ranjith observed closely, occasionally jotting down notes. The room remained quiet except for Aditya's voice. It was a critical moment in the investigation, and every word mattered.

As the conversation continued, it became clear that Inspector Ranjith and Ananya were determined to uncover the truth behind the 'Shivan's Pride' movement, its objectives, and the recent events that had brought it into the spotlight. Aditya, too, was resolute in his quest for justice and recognition for those who deserved.

'So Aditya, do you doubt anyone's role in the missing case of your father and his friend?' Asked Ranjith.

'Yes, I do. Two people and one among them has died in an accident but that was mysterious.'

'May we know who they are'? Asked the inspector.

'One is the former sarpanch of our village, Mr. Chinnappa who died mysteriously and another is Prakash Devan.'

'Are you sure, you are on record.' Stressed the inspector.

'I am very much sure. I also fear that he too might be killed if you don't take him to custody immediately and put him under continuous observation.'

'What proof you have to share with us.'

'My father went missing when I was eight years. I recollect moments with him so alive. If not in my father's lap, I could not fall into sleep. I used to wait everyday till my father was home and whatever and wherever he was, he used to return only for me. Days before my father and Vikram uncle went missing, I remember the conversation between my father and Vikram uncle. Every day they used to talk that they met Prakash Devan along with Chinnappa. They have been meeting them almost every day for at least fifteen days and one day they went missing. Only the scooter they used was found near the forest somewhere. But when the police at that time asked Prakash Devan, he said that it has been more than a month he met them. Suddenly a rumor popped up that my father and Vikram uncle escaped with a treasure.'

'Very brief and straight but how can an eight-year-old remember this.' Surprisingly asked the inspector.

'They had been talking about meetings with treasure, chinnappa and Prakash Devan and I thought of asking them in the morning who they were talking about all the night but my father never gave me time in the day. It continued for many days and suddenly when he disappeared, I think that got struck in my mind.'

'Did you inform anyone at that time?'

'No. My mother fell ill for months and I was with my granny. I think I didn't know what was happening but after few years I told them what I remembered but nothing could be done as we didn't know how to proceed.'

'Anything more to add to your statement?'

'Yes, around ten years before, I fought with Chinnappa to tell the truth about my father's missing mystery. I raged his house, held his throat, pulled him off his house and stabbed him on his face. I told him that in knew my father met him every day before he went missing and asked him why he said to police that he did not meet my father. He had no answer. I warned him that he will be killed if he doesn't share the truth. Just a month later he was found dead in his car.'

'So, what is the mystery in it?

'The witnesses observed his throat was slit, and the car that collided with the tree did not have any major damage nor was any mark of blood noticed on his head or chest. There was no post-mortem conducted. The police did not register a case and the body was cremated in few hours.'

'Ooh, what action did the police take?'

'His wife and his daughter filed a case against me. The police arrested me as a suspect. But luckily, I had been out of the village. I was in the capital city to participate in the state-level kabaddi tournament. They checked my records, visited the sports center and released me.'

'So how do you link this to the conspiracy?'

'It is just a speculation I have, that Chinnappa might have met Prakash Devan and told about the fight we had. If Chinnappa was eliminated, then no one knew what happened.'

'But doesn't Prakash Devan know that you were doubting him too?'

'No, never I expressed my doubt because he is a public figure and I also wanted to sort the things from Chinnappa first.'

'But do you believe your father got a treasure jar?' enquired the police.

'I really don't know but somehow rumours emerged that my father and his friend found one treasure spot in the forest and they say the jar was later seized by Chinnapa and Prakash Devan.'

'Did they hide it somewhere in any of your properties or house?'

'I don't think so. Immediately when they went missing, we offered the police, the villagers to search our house and asked them to trespass all our lands and the rice mill. A few did but could not find anything.'

'Do you believe, your father is alive?'

'No, I don't.'

'Is there a missing case filed at that time?'

'No, I don't think so.' Replied Aditya.

'Ananya, immediately check with the police station if there was a case filed on this missing.' Ordered Ranjith to Ananya.

'Prakash Devan is well off, he is very rich, why do you think he would risk?'

'This is what I am saying. There is a large conspiracy behind it. I am sure, he is the agent of the royal family. He is just ensuring that the treasure is not seen. Because if it is seen, then the entire story of Shivan's pride would be proven true. Once you reach a certain level of wealth, often it's your name and reputation that become even more valuable and sought after. The royal family cannot face the shame. And frankly, I am not sure this investigation too will go unbiased.'

Inspector Ranjith leaned back in his chair, contemplating Aditya's words carefully. 'You can trust us, Aditya,' he reassured. 'At least till now, we've had no external pressure affecting our work.'

Aditya, still wary, nodded but couldn't shake off his deep-seated suspicions. The room felt charged with tension, and the weight of unresolved mysteries hung heavily in the air. The inquiry conversation concluded with the statement from Aditya, 'To solve this mystery is my calling.'

The next step of the investigation was to enquire about Prakash Devan. The inspector Ranjith, had done his homework thoroughly. He came to know there were no police cases filed for the missing cases of Raghava and Vikram, nor the death of Chinnappa. Ranjith meticulously examined Prakash Devan's profile before calling him in for questioning and worked rigorously to extract all the personal and financial information to connect the dots of illegal money flow. One day Prakash Devan was summoned to visit the DIG office to cooperate with the investigation.

'Welcome, Mr. Prakash Devan,' Ranjith greeted him confidently. He maintained eye contact his gaze unwavering as if trying to read Prakash Devan's thoughts.

'Thank you, Inspector,' Prakash Devan replied, although he appeared to be suffering from a minor cough. He cleared his throat, an involuntary sign of nervousness.

'Are you feeling all right?' Ranjith inquired, his tone softening slightly to convey a sense of concern.

'I've been unwell for a few days, but I can cooperate,' Prakash Devan responded, his voice strained.

'We've got your health reports, and I must say, you seem healthier than me,' Ranjith remarked sarcastically, an ironic smile playing at the corner of his lips.

'Yes, I make sure not to skip my daily exercise routine and never deviate from my diet,' Prakash Devan replied, trying to maintain a composed demeanor.

'That's impressive. But what about when you're out of town and staying in hotels?' Ranjith probed, leaning back slightly in his chair.

'In those cases, I prefer to walk at least five miles and depend more on veggies and fruits,' Prakash Devan explained, his fingers nervously tapping the armrest of his chair.

'We should all learn discipline from you, sir,' the inspector commented, with Ananya nodding in agreement. Ranjith's tone softened, attempting to put Prakash Devan at ease.

'You're being quite sarcastic,' Prakash Devan noted, raising an eyebrow and locking eyes with Ranjith.

'No, I assure you, I mean it,' Ranjith replied, offering a subtle nod of respect.

'All right then,' Prakash Devan said, accepting the comment, his shoulders relaxing ever so slightly.

'Now, Mr. Prakash Devan, let's get to the point,' Ranjith said, taking a sip of water from a glass on the table, his eyes never leaving Prakash Devan. Prakash Devan nodded in acknowledgment.

'When did you first become involved in the Shivan's Pride movement?' Ranjith asked, leaning forward slightly, his fingers steeped in front of him.

'I joined in the 1980s,' Prakash Devan responded, his gaze fixed on a point in the room.

'I'm not asking when the movement itself started, but when you became associated with it,' Ranjith clarified, his brows furrowing slightly.

'That would be in 1985,' Prakash Devan confirmed, a flicker of nostalgia in his eyes.

'Is it true that your first visit was during the hunger strike led by Raghava and Chinnappa?' Ranjith inquired, studying Prakash Devan's facial expressions closely.

'Yes, you seem to have gathered accurate information,' Prakash Devan replied, intrigued but guarded.

'I went through the register, which had events listed chronologically, and I believe it was maintained by Raghava,' Ranjith explained, reaching for a file on the table.

'Yes, Raghava was responsible for documenting the minutes of all happenings,' Prakash Devan confirmed, his fingers lightly tapping the armrest again.

'Surprisingly, Raghava and Chinnappa, decided to give up the strike after just two days and it happened soon after your arrival, even though they didn't know who you were until you reached,' Ranjith remarked, his tone probing.

'Yes, but after I arrived, the local police and the media introduced me to my various successful campaigns, which boosted their confidence,' Prakash Devan explained, his gaze shifting to the table.

'Several prominent figures, including the Deputy Chief Minister, MLA, and local politicians, attempted to halt the hunger strike, but only you managed to achieve this within an hour,' Ranjith pointed out, leaning forward even more.

'At that time, they didn't trust the politicians, so they saw me as a ray of hope,' Prakash Devan replied, his hands clasped tightly together.

'Raghava and a few others initiated the hunger strike, and later Chinnappa joined them. Both were side by side at the protest area. Are you aware of this?' Ranjith asked a hint of scrutiny in his eyes.

'Yes, we have press coverage that shows them together,' Prakash Devan acknowledged, his fingers now intertwined.

'Raghava was the one who began the strike, and Chinnappa followed. Did you know that?' Ranjith questioned, his gaze unyielding.

'No, I was not aware of that,' Prakash Devan replied, his expression shifting to one of surprise.

'But it is true, as documented,' Ranjith stated, flipping through the file in front of him.

'It might be, that Raghava was a remarkable leader who worked without seeking any position. He was focused on our cause,' Prakash Devan said, his voice reflecting respect.

'It's also recorded that you offered juice to Chinnappa first, and he immediately accepted. Then, when Raghava and others hesitated, both you and Chinnappa pressured them to accept. Is this true?' Ranjith asked, his eyes locked on Prakash Devan.

'I don't recall that specific incident,' Prakash Devan replied, his forehead creasing in thought.

'It's not a minor incident to forget, Mr. Prakash Devan,' Ranjith remarked, leaning back and observing Prakash Devan's reaction. Prakash Devan's pretension that he forgot this major incident strengthened Ranjith's doubts.

'Under such circumstances, events can unfold spontaneously. We often focus more on the objective than on the processes. What you've described might have occurred, but I don't deny it. However, what are you trying to imply?' Prakash Devan questioned, his gaze returning to meet Ranjith's.

'I might call it reconstructing or rewinding, but let's just say I'm confirming the registered facts,' Ranjith said, his fingers drumming lightly on the table.

'No problem,' Prakash Devan replied, releasing a breath he seemed to have been holding.

'Now, Mr. Prakash Devan, before your association with the Shivan's Pride movement, what were your major achievements or projects?' Ranjith inquired, poised to delve deeper into Prakash Devan's past. As the conversation continued, the room seemed to grow colder, and the air thicker with tension.

'I protested against many environmental issues, worked for human rights, against child labor, and many. My life is meant for protesting against any wrong I come across,' Prakash Devan said, his voice steady but tinged with an underlying passion.

'Why do you think raising your voice at every small issue is important?' Ranjith asked, genuinely curious.

'In a democracy, the protest is inbuilt, but only a few understand it. Protesting or raising one's voice is not opposing; in a country like India, we need to shout to be heard, and this is what I am doing. I am shouting so that others may hear and act if they are capable,' Prakash Devan replied, his eyes reflecting his unwavering conviction.

'There were instances when you protested selectively or without much knowledge on the subject. For example, you filed a PIL on an educational institute for collecting high fees, but you overlooked others that collected even higher. Is that true?' Ranjith probed, a hint of skepticism in his voice.

'Yes, but partially. I spoke to all the institutions in that city, and everyone agreed to lower the fees the next year, but this institute did not respond properly. I requested them and explained the consequences of the school fees on the middle class, but they were reluctant,' Prakash Devan explained.

'However, no one dropped their fees the following year, and the court called your complaint a personal agenda,' Ranjith pointed out, his gaze unwavering.

'It happened, and it's unfortunate,' Prakash Devan admitted, his shoulders slumping slightly.

'There are many cases where you were indirectly involved. You filed many PILs in the name of your subordinates and friends,' Ranjith continued, scrutinizing Prakash Devan's reactions.

'No, they were inspired by my work and learned the art of activism,' Prakash Devan countered, his expression unwavering.

'But they might not have learned properly. More than fifty percent of the PILs were found irrelevant and driven by personal targets. Is there a way one can profit from this loophole? I am just curious,' Ranjith inquired, his eyes narrowing slightly.

'Every process has a loophole, of course, but I don't think people around me are like that,' Prakash Devan answered with a hint of defensiveness in his voice.

'You have also fought for prisoners' rights and the release of wrongfully convicted prisoners. I appreciate that. You have also received an award for that from some private institution, I guess,' Ranjith said, his tone softening slightly.

'Yes, it added more strength and confidence to me,' Prakash Devan said, a glimmer of pride in his eyes.

'I noticed the certificate; it was in 1985, the same year you started to associate with the Shivan's Pride movement,' Ranjith observed.

'Yes, the same year. I do remember it. I was honored by one of the central ministers,' Prakash Devan replied, his posture straightening.

'Do you know who sponsored the event?' Ranjith asked, his voice lowering.

'No, I don't,' Prakash Devan replied.

'It was sponsored by the royal family of the then Vijetha Mandala,' Ranjith dropped the revelation, watching for Prakash Devan's reaction.

'Is it! I was informed by some public relations officer of the institute and was told that the central minister would honor me. That's all I knew,' Prakash Devan said, his expression a mix of surprise and curiosity.

'You were once attacked by some unidentified people while you were protesting against an issue, and you were warned that you would be killed. We are impressed to know that you continued the fight,' Ranjith noted, acknowledging Prakash Devan's courage.

'That was the same we discussed; the management of the education institution attacked me,' Prakash Devan explained, his voice tinged with bitterness.

'But the police said there was no evidence,' Ranjith stated, raising an eyebrow.

'That was their incapability to find,' Prakash Devan retorted, his frustration evident.

'We were informed that once you were away from home, and your wife delivered a baby which died in just two days,' Ranjith said, his voice softening.

'Yes, it is the worst thing that ever happened to our family,' Prakash Devan admitted, his eyes welling up with sadness.

'How tough is your heart that you did not return immediately and followed the schedule exactly?' Ranjith probed, his gaze piercing.

'I had been work-oriented; if my schedule is disturbed, it affects many others who depended on me,' Prakash Devan replied, his voice breaking slightly.

'Such a champion of protests, how come you were silent when Raghava and Vikram went missing? Why was there no PIL filed against the police who refused to register a case?' Ranjith questioned, his tone accusatory.

'I don't know why I didn't act; maybe I got priorities,' Prakash Devan said, his voice faltering.

'You didn't care when your newborn baby died while you were at work. What more priorities does such a dedicated and healthy man might have had?' Ranjith pressed his voice hardening.

'How can you hold anyone responsible for not doing something that was not his duty? I might have been unwell at that time,' Prakash Devan defended, his eyes defiant.

'Your medical records show you are in perfect health, and you also didn't have any medical problems till now,' Ranjith countered, his tone relentless.

'So, what do you want to conclude?' Prakash Devan asked, his voice weary.

'We only want your admission that you met Raghava and Vikram almost every day for a week before they died,' Ranjith stated firmly, pushing a file forward that presented all the financial transactions and events in chronological order.

'You can't force me to lie,' Prakash Devan protested, his hands gripping the edges of the table.

'You will admit it, Prakash Devan, you will. But what we want you to reveal is who else was involved in this conspiracy,' Ranjith declared, his gaze unwavering.

Prakash Devan sat back in his chair, contemplating his next move, as Ranjith and Ananya left the room, leaving him to tackle the weight of his choices during the break.

As the interrogation team was back and took their seats, the room grew silent. Prakash Devan found himself cornered, his every defense crumbling in the face of overwhelming evidence. The relentless questioning, supported by a meticulously compiled dossier of documents and financial transactions, had left him with no option but to surrender and lay bare the dark secrets he had been guarding.

The room, once echoing with heated exchanges, now hung heavy with an intense sense of defeat. Prakash Devan, who had been a renowned activist, stood there with a heavy heart, his usually resolute behavior shattered. The then personal secretary to the central minister of environment and forest, the then MLA, and even the former superintendent of police were implicated alongside him. It was a shocking revelation that sent shockwaves throughout the region.

The plot's intricacies were both complicated and wicked, far surpassing anyone's expectations. At first glance, it appeared to be a meticulously crafted tale, but upon unraveling the execution, one couldn't help but marvel at the precision of the laid plans and the vast sums of money involved. The royal family, once considered a symbol of tradition and authority, had masterminded this elaborate scheme. Their objective was to protect a closely guarded secret—a hidden treasure that had the potential to rewrite history and prove the authenticity of the Shivan's Pride movement. The personal secretary, a trusted aide to one of the central ministers, had played the role of the chief conspirator, orchestrating a web of deceit and manipulation.

The revelation of how Raghava and Vikram met their demise sent shivers down the spines of everyone who heard it.

Prakash Devan said, 'Vikram and Raghava had approached us one day with a treasure jar and secured it in my guest house. They trusted us so deeply that they hadn't even disclosed it to their family members. Of course, Vikram had no family. Every day, Vikram, Raghava, Chinnappa and I, gathered at my house to strategize how to reveal this treasure to the world, to prove its existence and thereby honor the soldiers' sacrifice. We were pretending to lag for a few days until the MLA who was on a foreign visit would come back. The day when the MLA came and joined the meeting Both Raghava and Vikram were taken aback by the MLA's unexpected presence. The MLA initiated the discussion, imploring both of them to become part of a sinister conspiracy. To this, they fervently disagreed. In their frustration, they retreated into the room where the treasure was concealed, only to discover it had vanished. Panic and anger took over, leading them to attack us. It was the MLA who fired the fatal shots, and later, in an attempt to conceal the heinous act, we burnt the bodies to ashes. To further mislead the public, we left the scooter on the roadside of the forest towards Jhagaram.'

The police Officer nearly stood up his astonishment evident. 'Conspiracy, you say? What kind of conspiracy are we talking about, Prakash Devan?'

Prakash Devan glanced around cautiously before responding, 'Well, it's a rather covert arrangement, you see. This conspiracy revolves around a well-kept secret pact that has been in place for quite some time.'

Intrigued, the Police Officer probed further, 'A secret pact? Could you elaborate, Prakash?'

Speaking in hushed tones, Prakash Devan explained, 'Of course. The heart of this conspiracy lies in a particular agreement, a sort of unwritten rule. It dictates that should anyone stumble upon a hidden treasure the loot is to be meticulously divided into two equal portions.'

The Police Officer, raising an eyebrow, questioned, 'Divided? Into two halves? Who gets these portions?'

Nodding solemnly, Prakash Devan affirmed, 'Indeed. The first half, the lion's share, is reserved for a select group, including myself, Chinnappa, the MLA, and a handful of individuals who hold certain expectations within the system. They anticipate a share. The other half, well, it's set aside for someone with even greater influence.'

Eager to know more, the Police Officer continued, 'And who might that be, Prakash?'

Pausing, as if choosing his words carefully, Prakash Devan revealed, 'The other half, my friend, is the personal secretary to the central minister.'

The revelation of this conspiracy shook the very foundations of power and authority in the region. It shattered the trust of the people in those they had considered their guardians. The once-respected figures now faced the consequences of their actions, condemned by the very system they had sworn to protect.

The police were also able to confiscate the brass jar from the mango orchid of Prakash Devan that acted as concrete evidence of everything that happened.

The conviction of these prominent individuals sent a clear message: no one, regardless of their status or influence, was above the law. It served as a stark reminder that justice would always find a way, even in the face of the most carefully crafted conspiracies. The region, the erstwhile Vijetha mandala, now aware of the truth, had to grapple with the repercussions of this revelation—a turning point that would redefine its future.

The exposure of the conspiracy left no room for debate regarding the sacrifice of the twenty-one soldiers. In the face of overwhelming evidence, the government found itself with no other viable option but to officially declare the day of their sacrifice as 'Shivans' Divas'. As a mark of respect, the government extended the gesture further by granting the erstwhile kingdom of Vijetha Mandala a local holiday for all its businesses on this solemn day.

Recognizing the historical significance and the need to immortalize the soldiers' valor, the government pledged to include their heroic stories in the official textbooks used for educating the nation's youth. As a practical demonstration of their commitment, the government also earmarked a specific fund dedicated to preserving and commemorating this chapter of history. The Government appreciated the persistent efforts of many activists and stressed that people should continue to protest for their rights and only then it is called a democracy.

To ensure that the sacrifices of these brave soldiers were never forgotten, the government established a tradition where a designated representative from the government would attend the annual ceremony held in their honor. This act served as an emotional reminder of the debt of gratitude owed to those who had laid down their lives for a noble cause.

Furthermore, the government took a proactive stance in managing the treasure hunt. A panel was established to ensure the meticulous and controlled exploration of the hidden riches. This panel consisted of esteemed members, each contributing their expertise to the endeavor. It included the Archaeological Survey of India, responsible for preserving and understanding the historical significance of any findings; a Forest Department officer, who could guide the exploration through the dense wilderness; and the Managing Trustee of the Shiva's Pride movement, ensuring the soldiers' legacy was respected throughout the process.

Moreover, the judiciary played a crucial role in determining the distribution of the treasure's spoils. In a landmark decision, the court adjudicated the division of the discovered treasure between the government and the erstwhile kingdom of Vijetha Mandala. The court's verdict was based on a fair and logical approach, considering the investments made by the state in the treasure hunt and its ongoing supervision.

The court decreed that, as the state would commit its valuable resources to the challenging task of treasure hunting and overseeing the process, it was entitled to a ten percent share of any findings in the initial year. To reflect the state's continued commitment and dedication to this endeavor, the court also ruled that this share would incrementally increase by ten percent each subsequent year. This progressive arrangement would persist until the state's share reached a substantial sixty-percent of any discovered treasure, ensuring a balanced and equitable distribution of the recovered wealth.

The S Code mystery

From the very year, 1945, when the treasure was buried by the soldiers, some adventurers and enthusiasts tried to decode the puzzled story of treasure. In the process, what every new adventurer and a new enthusiast did was to meet the family members of those twenty-one soldiers. The families and the extended families of those soldiers were traced to get first-hand information and to listen to the code and inquire if any more clues persisted with them. Except for the youngest soldier, the families of the twenty brave soldiers were traced and those families became well-known across the erstwhile region of Vijetha Mandala. Those families too grew tired of the constant visits from curious folks who wanted to hear the code repeated over and over again. To put an end to the never-ending requests, they decided to write down what they had heard directly from the soldiers and wrote it on their walls.

Upon reaching Rishi Pahar Mountain, we beseeched Lord Shiva for his divine aid. Answering our plea, Lord Shiva appeared with a bow as high as the sky and concealed the treasures using the mountain-sized massive serpent as his arrow. The serpent clutched all the treasure jars with its fangs, and upon Lord Shiva's command, it sailed through the forest, secreting away the treasures deep under the soil, with the iron ring a few inches below the ground.

However, there was still one mystery left: the family of the youngest soldier.

From the little hints and pieces of information the other twenty soldiers had given before they died, it seemed that the youngest among them was the one who had guided the team in hiding the treasure and had also created the complicated code protecting it. Many tried to find the family of this young soldier, but they couldn't. It appeared that the family had disappeared on the same day the soldiers came back home. There was one person who had seen closely what happened that day, a neighbor of the young soldier's family. Through that person what everyone knew was that the young soldier who returned home from the forest after being poisoned, revealed the code, wrote it on his sister's slate, and made everyone who gathered around mug it up like a hymn. Later, he gave a leather bag to his family and asked them to leave the kingdom fearing the king but before they left, the soldier whispered something to his family. After the family left the kingdom, some tried to trace them but they were not found.

Aditya returned to Jhagaram after the court's judgment. The villages of the former Vijetha Mandala region organized a grand welcome for their leader, Aditya. He was both relieved by the verdict and proud that the mystery surrounding his father's death had finally been solved. It took a week for the excitement of the people to subside, but Aditya now faced a new challenge: finding the remaining treasure jars.

During that time of Aditya's life - from unearthing the treasure jar and fighting to solve the mystery of his father's demise - his wife with her child had been staying with her parents only for the reason that Aditya had no time for the family and had been fighting against many odds and coordination with institutions. During that tenure itself, his granny died because of her old age.

After the court judgment and after Aditya returned to Jhagaram with his wife and the child, the death anniversary of Aditya's grandmother was approaching, and it had to be organized that month. He needed to make arrangements and visit all the relatives to distribute the invitation cards for the death anniversary.

On the day of the anniversary, after the ceremony had ended, a tradition required that the deceased's personal valuables be opened in the presence of all the heirs and distributed among them. As Raghava was the sole heir, the shelf holding his late grandmother's precious belongings had to be opened by him on that day. Everyone knew it contained two golden bracelets and four golden rings that had belonged to her late husband. On that evening, after the relatives and the guests had left the ceremony, Aditya visited the shelf alone and when Aditya opened the shelf that had been gathering dust in the corner of the prayer room, he was astounded. Inside, he found a leather bag filled with gold coins and a long, sturdy, and zig-zag patterned gold ornament adorned with pearls in an unusual shape. The hook of the chain was shaped like a snake's head. The gold coins were identical to those he had seen in the treasure jar. Alongside the leather bag, he discovered another small box containing his late grandfather's bracelets, golden rings, and a locket. He examined the coins, they resembled the coins that were in the brass jar and the locket had the text carved in a text read '**To my loving sister Shivani**'. Shivani was his Granny's name. Suddenly, he recalled the story of the youngest soldier who had given his family - his mother and the younger little sister, a leather bag before they went into exile. It dawned on him that his grandmother was the sister of that young soldier, the mastermind behind the plan to safely bury the treasure and create the code that had mystified everyone.

Aditya was convinced that the code lay hidden within that zig zag-shaped gold ornament. As he counted the pearls adorning the ornament, he found there were twenty-one of them, each equidistant from the next. When placed on the floor, it resembled a snake's curves, with each pearl taking its place on every curve. One end of the structure resembled the head of the snake and another end had one perpendicular end flatted to resemble a mountain. The length of the perpendicular structure at the end was equal to the length of each curve. It seemed to have been made from the cuff bracelets made of gold. Aditya didn't take long to decipher the code. The snake-shaped ornament facilitated Aditya's rapid deciphering of the code. Guided not only by the cryptic clues given by the soldiers but also armed with knowledge about three pivotal locations where the treasure had been discovered—the towering pillar, Naagam's beehive spot, and the location highlighted by his father's friend, Vikram.

Aditya hurried to the GOST, the troop that celebrated and spread the bravery of the soldiers' sacrifice. He sought out the leader of the troop, Ravidasa, and inquired about the name of the youngest soldier.

'What is the name of the youngest soldier?' Aditya asked eagerly.

Ravidasa responded, 'His name is 'Vijaya.''

Aditya pressed further, 'Is it just Vijaya, or does he have any other names, like a middle name or something?'

Ravidasa clarified, 'It's actually 'Vijaya Raghava.''

Aditya's anxiety eased as he obtained this vital piece of information, and he returned with a sense of purpose. Consolidating all the stories, and probabilities with the information and comprehension, Aditya rightly imagined what all happened with Vijaya Raghava, the youngest soldier, and the code he designed embedded in a puzzled story.

In a secluded spot near the Rishi Pahar Mountain, Vijaya Raghava, the young and resourceful soldier, knelt down and used a sharp stone on the damp soil to sketch out his plan. His fellow soldiers gathered around, their attention fixed on the makeshift map taking shape before them.

On the damp soil, Vijaya Raghava started by outlining the majestic Rishi Pahar Mountain and carefully marked the location of the revered Lord Shiva's temple on the mountain. With precision, he drew a long, straight line extending from the temple and etched a zigzag pattern along the line that resembled a winding snake.

'We follow this straight line,' he began, 'and at every five hundred steps, one of us will veer off to the side, walking another five hundred steps, and burying the treasure jar under the nearest Arjuna tree. If the first soldier goes right, the second one goes left, maintaining the snake-like pattern and burying the treasure at the curves. The layout of the treasure mimics the winding form of a snake, with each treasure spot approximately half a kilometer away from the central line. And not to forget to place the iron ring just half a foot below the ground' said Vijaya Raghava and took out his thin golden cuff bracelet that coiled his wrist four rounds and the sacred beaded thread that rounded his neck. He wanted to depict his plan more concrete and wend that thin wired bracelet in the zig zag pattern that resembled a snake with twenty-one curves.

At every curve, he embedded a bead, the entire structure acting as a key to the code. Also at one end of the bracelet, he stabbed it to make the face of a snake and at the other end, he wend it perpendicular to resemble the mountain. He ensured that the perpendicular structure length and the length of each curve is equal.

His fellow soldiers exchanged approving glances, impressed by the simplicity and effectiveness of the plan.

Eager to ensure a complete understanding, one of the soldiers clarified, ' The first spot is aligned in line with the temple at nearly five hundred steps from it and the remaining treasure locations are strategically positioned at the bends of the snake pattern, each approximately half a kilometer from the central line, which originates from the Shiva temple, right?'

Vijaya Raghava nodded with a grin, 'That's absolutely right. And there's another reason for this choice of five hundred meters distance is because it is the length of the Rishi Pahar Mountain. This central line is also chosen because it is the shortest route to many nearby villages. If you take any side path along the way, you'll eventually reach a village where you can seek guidance to reach your destination.'

In one of the border villages, Vijaya Raghava's family included his mother and a seven-year-old younger sister Shivani. On that deadly evening, when he finally got back home from the forest, looking very tired and worried, Shivani burst into tears. Her crying was so loud that it made the neighbors worried, and a few of them came over to see if something was wrong.

Vijaya Raghava, with a heavy heart, told them the scary story of what had happened and how they had been trapped. He revealed the code to everyone gathered around and even wrote it on the slate and made everyone repeat it so that it was mugged up. It was through that gathering that the code passed on like a hymn without deviation. Vijaya Raghava reiterated that the twenty-one treasure jars were meant for the people of Vijetha Mandala, and he desperately hoped that not even one jar would end up in the wrong hands.

Later, he begged his mother and Shivani to leave the kingdom right away, fearing the king. Before his family left, he took out a leather bag and gifted it to his sister and whispered 'The bag has some gold coins for you to survive. There is an object in the bag that explains the code more clearly which you should not show to anyone unless you feel they are worthy of deciphering the code and utilizing the treasure for the benefit of the kingdom, otherwise, just keep it as my memory. And never reveal your identity as my family in your life, someday someone might torture you and your future families to death to reveal the treasure code.'

Sadly, their time together was short. The soldiers who were loyal to the king wasted no time and took the youngest soldier away to the castle. Tragically, by the early hours of the next morning, the body arrived back for cremation.

Epilogue: What is S code

Srirangam Srinivasa Rao, a modern and highly influential Telugu writer, in his celebrated work, 'Mahaprasthanam,' said

'It is not the grandeur of the palanquins

That the kings were carried in

But rather, history lies in the tales and toils

Of those palanquin bearers'

'The S code' is one such story of palanquin bearers.

But what is the S code? The obvious response could be 'The Shivan's code' if not 'The Soldiers' code' or 'The Serpent's Code' but it doesn't resonate at some corner of our thoughts that The S code may also be The Shivani's Code.

Upon the soldier Vijaya Raghava's plea, his mother embarked on a daunting journey with young Shivani by her side. The journey through the dense forest stretched for two long days – How threatening could their journey have been?

They headed to her brother's home, sought refuge, and made a fresh start – What could it take for a seven-year girl to be a refugee?

Years passed, and at the age of twelve, Shivani had to bid farewell to her mother. What profound grief must have weighed upon her heart, having lost everyone in her family at such a tender age!

Shivani was adopted by her uncle, who arranged her marriage to a man from Jhagaaram village. What challenges must she have faced to step into another family and embark on a new beginning?

Shivani had known profound loss since her childhood. Her father had perished in a battle, serving the British - her brother, Vijaya Raghava fell for the treacherous plan of the prince - her mother's departure had occurred when she was just a child of twelve - grief revisited her when she lost her husband in the treasure hunt at the age of twenty-five - the most devastating blow came with the untimely demise of her one and only son, Raghava.

However, through the many trials life hurled at Shivani, she had to toil tirelessly for her family. She managed to amass a respectable fortune for her son's future. Even after his demise, she faced the harsh consequences of life with resilience, rebuilding her home after it had been ransacked. Through it all, she steadfastly guarded her true identity, never revealing that she was the sister of the great young soldier Vijaya Raghava for the only reason that it created trouble for her family. Proudly she even gifted a decent amount to her grandson Aditya when he started the business of sanitary ware in the town.

She dedicated herself to the toil of the agricultural fields for as long as her body could bear the burden. When the rigors of fieldwork became too difficult, she dedicated herself to crafting beedis, the desi cigars, throughout the day but never stopped to work. Her unwavering work ethic persisted until she was confined to her bed.

How many such **S** codes went missing in history. They had no songs written for them, nor were their efforts considered as valor, and their hard work was taken for granted. Forget songs and celebration of their valor, their names are not known for they have been only called mother, sister, wife, and daughter. The S code is both Shivan's code and Shivani's code

Look around, at how many **S** codes happened yesterday and are happening at this moment!

www.ingramcontent.com/pod-product-compliance
Lightning Source LLC
LaVergne TN
LVHW041703070526
838199LV00045B/1184